LOVE'S MEASURE

Maisie Hampton

CHIVERS

THORNDIKE

This Large Print book is published by BBC Audiobooks Ltd, Bath, England and by Thorndike Press®, Waterville, Maine, USA.

Published in 2005 in the U.K. by arrangement with Robert Hale Ltd.

Published in 2005 in the U.S. by arrangement with Robert Hale Limited.

U.K. Hardcover ISBN 1–4056–3415–4 (Chivers Large Print)
U.K. Softcover ISBN 1–4056–3416–2 (Camden Large Print)
U.S. Softcover ISBN 0–7862–7850–1 (Buckinghams)

The text of this Large Print edition is unabridged.
Other aspects of the book may vary from the original edition.

Set in 16 pt. New Times Roman.

Printed in Great Britain on acid-free paper.

British Library Cataloguing in Publication Data available

Library of Congress Cataloging-in-Publication Data

Hampton, Maisie.
    Love's measure / by Maisie Hampton.
      p.   cm.
    "Thorndike Press large print Buckinghams."—T.p. verso.
    ISBN 0–7862–7850–1 (lg. print : sc : alk. paper)
    1. Guardian and ward—Fiction. 2. Teenage girls—Fiction.
    3. Nobility—Fiction. 4. Large type books. I. Title.
PR6058.A556L68 2005
823'.92—dc22   2005012124

For Betty King,
Kay, Tom and Lynda Muirhead

Special thanks to Peter and Valerie, Lois, sisters and brother-in-law; and particularly to Jo Haenan Blackwell for her guidance on equine matters. I have received valued help from Hal Coomer, support and encouragement from friends in the Cotswold Writers' Circle, and from my own Canadian *ancien combattant,* of course.

CHAPTER ONE

London, February 1812

There was no doubt about it. His recent succession presaged a radical change to his life. He thought with pleasure of his friends' celebration for him at the Cocoa Tree last evening, and of the inevitable avalanche of invitations to salons and social functions—far more for a bachelor earl than hitherto for a bachelor viscount. The note from Sir Henry Nancarrow, his godfather and family attorney, summoning him to an urgent consultation, contained the words '. . . *your inheritance is in a devilish mess.*' It was as if a pall had been cast over his expectations, making him anxious to see Sir Henry without delay.

Guy, seventh Earl of Adversane, left his club at St James's and walked briskly to hail a hackney-coach in Piccadilly. A strong wind whipped the skirts of his long mourning-coat, and the darkening sky suddenly dispersed giant raindrops which hardened to hailstones spattering the streets. He held on to his hat as people surged by to seek shelter. Alongside him, wheels crunched to a stop on the icy mass, and a coach door flung open. From within, a hand, gloved in embroidered pink kid, beckoned him to board. Avidly, he leapt into the vehicle to escape the hail now falling with fury, and found himself staring into the rouged face of Lady Charlotte Cotterell, the darling of Almack's. He closed the door before raising his hat, shook from it the clinging water drops, and placed it on the hatrack along with his cane.

'Tell Mr Swallow, my coachman, where you wish to go, Guy. He's attending the horses and could hear you from the window.'

'But surely, Charlotte, it's more important that you continue to your destination. Simply stop at the top of Piccadilly where I can find a hackney-coach. Your arrival was most timely and rescued me from the hail.'

At that moment, a flurry of icy pellets battered the windows. The storm showed no sign of abating.

'You cannot walk abroad in weather like this!' she exclaimed.

Guy had to agree with her. He opened the window and called to the coachman: 'Could you take me to Chancery Lane, Mr Swallow?'

'Aye, my lord, soon as I've calmed the 'orses,' was the reply.

Guy nodded and closed the window. 'Thank you, Charlotte.'

Her smile broadened. 'Come, sit here, Guy,' she said, indicating a place beside her in the dark recess of the coach. 'I infer you are going to Chancery Lane about your inheritance.'

He swallowed. 'Yes. It's a saddening

procedure which reminds me of my loss.'

She moved closer, placing his arm under her silk cape and holding his hand to her bosom.

'Guy, I'll not let you grieve,' she whispered, her lips seeking his. Her kiss was light, exploratory. Suddenly, as the coach jolted and surged forward, Guy turned and kissed her long and hard, again and again, with a passion barely understood except that it relieved his grief and guilt. Loosing his hold, he paused; but her provocative response demanded continuance and gasping for breath, he released her abruptly as they entered Chancery Lane. The rain had stopped. He reached for the check-string, took up his hat and cane, and sprang from the coach as it slowed. He looked back but once. She was at the window, perplexed and replacing her bonnet. He raised his hat in farewell, turned into Sword Alley and entered a tall building to keep his appointment with Sir Henry. He bounded up the stairs two at a time, pausing on the first landing to withdraw a kerchief. Pressing it to his mouth, he wiped away the carmine left there after his fierce kissing of Lady Charlotte.

Since his return to London after his father's funeral in Hampshire, Lady Charlotte had sought him, offering consolation. He had always been ready to flirt with her, but she was inclined to favour those above the rank of viscount. He was aware that his succession assured her interest. The clutching and fumbling in the coach did not sit well with him and he wondered who was the more compromised by the incident.

One thing was certain: he needed to isolate himself and mourn his father's passing. It might make amends for those years in London when he had deliberately absented himself from his home. Even now his face burned with shame in thinking of Alice Brogan, a groom's daughter from the estate. During vacations from his academic tutorials at Oxford, Alice instructed him in the arts of seduction, enjoyed clandestinely in closets throughout the house.

He had thought himself in the throes of delirious first love, and the attachment continued until discovering that he was sharing Alice's favours with others on the estate. Appalled by the perfidy, he abruptly ended the affair and removed himself to London, with no explanation given or demanded. Subsequent visits to his home were infrequent and of short duration, but he came to regret the circumstances that forced him to leave the great Adversane estate in his ailing father's hands.

The smell of burnt sealing-wax assailed him as he entered the attorney's chambers. The scratching of quill upon parchment paper ceased momentarily as the scriveners looked up to see who had entered. The chief clerk, with a bow of recognition, escorted him to the library.

'Lord Adversane, Sir Henry,' he announced.

Sir Henry placed his quill in a standish, and rose from a table which was covered in documents and scrolls. He came towards Guy and bowed before offering his hand.

'My Lord Adversane, we are honoured by your presence.'

'Come now, Sir Henry,' said Guy, shaking his hand, 'omit the formal address. You have called me "Guy" ever since my baptism.'

'That was some twenty-seven years ago,' replied Sir Henry, his expression sombre. 'A blessed occasion for your parents, now *both* sadly departed. Your father was my good friend. I shall miss him, and my visits to Adversane.'

'They must not cease!' exclaimed Guy. 'Come as often as you wish. Nothing has changed!'

Sir Henry shook his head. 'If only that were so,' he said quietly. 'You must form your own establishment, dear boy.'

After handing the chief clerk his topcoat, hat and cane, Guy seated himself beside Sir Henry at the table.

'Is all this to do with father's probate?' Guy asked, indicating the mass of papers in front of Sir Henry.

Sir Henry nodded, hunched his shoulders and gave a massive sigh. 'I fear so.'

'Are there complications?'

'I fear so.'

'Do they affect the inheritance?'

'I fear so.' Sir Henry turned to unlock a tantalus on a cabinet beside him. 'There are things you should know which may be a grim surprise to you. You will need an exceedingly large brandy, Guy.'

'I fear so,' said Guy softly, as Sir Henry began to dispense the drinks into two goblets set by the tantalus.

Pinpricks of anxiety coursed through Guy as he pondered Sir Henry's words. He stretched his memory to recall anything amiss at the interment of his father in the graveyard at Adversane two months ago; but he could think of nothing. Through the numbness of grief and devastation at his father's unexpected demise, he had been comforted by relatives, friends and neighbours. He was particularly touched by the devotion shown by tenants and staff of the estate. There was no reason to doubt their sincerity.

With his sister, the Lady Elizabeth Dallimore, he had ensured that the funeral was conducted with due ceremony and grandeur. Sir Henry must be mistaken, he decided; but he marked Sir Henry's frowning absorption in pouring the drinks, his lined face unrelentingly mumpish.

There was a tense silence as both sipped their brandy. Then Guy said:

'Sir Henry, do not conjure pretty words to

disguise the truth of my position. Tell me of these complications with the candour I expect of you.'

Sir Henry took a deep draught from his goblet. 'There is no doubt that with the death of the sixth Earl of Adversane, as his only son you inherit as seventh Earl with the courtesy title Viscount Saxenford. That's a start. No complications there.'

'Then what is the nature of these other complications?'

'Financial.'

'I rather dreaded to hear you say that.'

Sir Henry sighed. 'You have been living for many years in the family house in Hanover Square in receipt of moneys from your father, and the costs of upkeep and staffing of the house were also borne by him.'

'That is true. Father did not wish the house unoccupied.'

'All met with borrowed money.'

'Borrowed?'

Sir Henry waved a sheaf of papers. 'Promissory notes, Guy, not yet redeemed.'

Guy frowned. 'Is it not possible to redeem some, at least?'

'No. Now let us consider Adversane.'

Guy shifted in his chair, crossed and uncrossed his legs and found difficulty in keeping a steady hand on his glass. 'Please do not tell me financial troubles exist there!'

'No pretty words, Guy. The estate is in a

mess.'

Guy gulped his brandy and leaned on the table, his hands clapped to his forehead. Moments passed before he said: 'What must I do?'

'Several things,' said Sir Henry, replenishing Guy's glass. 'It's my opinion something irregular is going on at Adversane. There's financial cheating and systematic plundering of the assets. You must investigate your father's steward, Mr Hynde Hallam, who seems to have usurped the position of land agent.'

Guy sat upright. He engaged Sir Henry with a direct gaze.

'I have not been the ideal son, Sir Henry,' he said. 'During my rare visits to Adversane, usually accompanied by guests, I allowed little opportunity for serious talks with father on estate matters. On the surface, everything appeared to be in order, which was the case when I attended the funeral. Your observations underline my shortcomings. My grief is compounded by the knowledge that time did not permit father to hear my reassurance and commitment to maintain all that he held dear. Guilt is a companion that lurks from sunrise and sees me to my bed, Sir Henry. I can only assuage it by pledging myself to rectify any immoderation at Adversane, to clear those debts and any smears attaching to our name.' He paused, then added: 'I wish I could have spoken thus to father.'

Sir Henry's expression lightened as he fingered some documents.

'He always had undiminished faith in you, Guy.'

At this Guy suffered a strange constriction in his throat and, in an effort to return to realities, asked:

'Are there any assets whatsoever?'

'The home farm flourishes as do the splendid Adversane greys at stud. There are some West Indian investments that may keep you afloat for a while.' Sir Henry sighed heavily as he continued: 'Apart from the estate house there are two other properties owned outright by the earldom. One is the London house, which you should lease immediately and thus derive income, while you move permanently to Adversane.'

'That shall be done; and the other property?'

'Ah, that is the manor house on the western boundary of Adversane. A Tudor delight.'

Guy shrugged. 'I am unaware of its existence.'

'Then you should visit it at the earliest opportunity. I have discovered an anomaly. The manor house is entailed to the earldom and cannot be sold. Adversane House is not entailed and can be sold if need be. By the same token, it is vulnerable to claims by debtors should bankruptcy ensue.'

'Is there a danger of that?'

Sir Henry pursed his lips. 'If you take up residence at Adversane House and are seen to be concerned in management of the estate, this may satisfy minor debtors and give them hope of settlement.'

'Could the manor house be leased, as we intend to lease the London house?'

'The manor house is already under a long lease. The quarterly rent is assured.'

'Who is the lessee?'

'A valued friend of mine and of your father. The brave and courageous Captain Sir John Stapleford, RN.'

'But wasn't he captured by the French in the Walcheren disaster?'

'The same gentleman. He engaged a French squadron threatening the Scheldt, and his gallant action saved a ship of the line and her crew. He is a hero, with accolades to come and we pray for his release or escape.'

'Then we are honoured to have such a neighbour, and I will personally see that the manor house is properly maintained during his imprisonment.'

Sir Henry nodded approval. 'You will find maps and documents in the estate office at Adversane. I advise you to take possession of them and keep them under lock and key. This will show the staff that you are serious in your undertaking.'

'I shall do so, Sir Henry.'

There was a silence. Guy turned to a window and looked out at grimy rooftops massed against a threatening sky. Somewhere a bell tolled, its mournful peal enhancing his sense of failure. He drained his glass.

'The position is crystal clear. Be assured, from this moment I pledge myself to Adversane. Please lease the London house, reserving for my occasional use the lower apartment.'

Sir Henry nodded. 'Let me know your conclusions about Adversane, and advise me if you need funds to cover a short-fall.'

'Thank you. I shall be in touch as soon as possible,' said Guy, rising. 'Now I should be on my way.'

Sir Henry rose and tugged at a bell pull, summoning Mr Bodmin, the chief clerk, who was instructed to bring Guy's coat, hat and cane. After donning them, Guy regarded himself in a large looking-glass placed on a wall near the door. His high-tied black stock and mourning-coat with its sable collar contrasted with his white silk waistcoat. The sobriety of his appearance matched his mood. When he had leapt from Lady Charlotte's coach earlier that morning, he perceived it as a gesture to escape his past. He would surrender the beau, the man about town, for a life of dedication to his inheritance. If that meant leaving London and moving to the country, then so be it.

11

He shook Sir Henry's hand again, and was about to open the door when Sir Henry spoke.

'One moment, Guy. You have such a positive approach to this catalogue of calamities, that I feel you could sustain one more encumbrance.'

Frowning, Guy turned. Sir Henry smiled. 'A likely diversion from the others. Our brave sailor, Sir John, being assigned active duties in the naval wars, appointed your father guardian of his daughter. Proximity was a factor in his choice, since they live in the manor house. Your father has overseen her welfare since Sir John's capture. As heir and successor, I feel you are bound to assume the guardianship until her father returns, or until Miss Sophia May Stapleford reaches her majority.'

'Miss Sophia May Stapleford!' sputtered Guy. 'Her guardian! Devil take it, Sir Henry, for how long?'

'Not for long. She's nineteen years of age.' Sir Henry's eyes twinkled. 'She's a comely little filly, they say, though somewhat wild.'

'Somewhat wild?'

'Your father appointed tutors, engaged a personal maid, supplied a small gig and mare, and gave her a black horse which she has been known to ride bareback.'

'Bareback!' Guy gasped.

'And astride.'

'Astride!'

'She adopts the riding skills of gypsies who

come to the estate.'

'Gypsies,' mouthed Guy, in shock.

Sir Henry smiled. 'The gypsies come and go. Miss Stapleford could not help but be aware of them. Your father was often amused by her escapades.'

It is unlikely they will amuse me, decided Guy. He touched his hat to Sir Henry, turned and left the chambers. 'What else?' he muttered as he stepped into Sword Alley Sir Henry had loaded a sufficiency of burdens upon him that morning. A comely little filly, indeed; and he her guardian! Lady Charlotte and her salon companions would shriek with laughter should they learn of it; but he hoped to be far away in Adversane within the week.

He turned into Chancery Lane and decided to walk to the Strand to clear his mind. A motley throng impeded him so he hailed a hackney-coach to take him to Hanover Square. He sank back with relief into the privacy of the coach, where he continued to reflect on his visit to Sir Henry. The matter of Miss Stapleford had struck him like a thunderbolt. A comely little filly, somewhat wild.

Confound it! How was he to cope with disorder in his finances and a disorderly ward!

The Manor House, Adversane Park, Hampshire, March 1812

The cobbled yard was deserted. Along the eastern horizon a margin of pale light banished the dark night. A glow came from the milking-shed, where only the cowmen were abroad at that early hour. There was no wind and the sky had a clearness almost equal to that of day.

Miss Sophia May Stapleford smiled to herself. 'Perfect,' she murmured, as she closed the yard gate and tiptoed to a stable in a back lane. Quietly, she drew back the bolt on the door. Jet, the black gelding, whinnied joyfully at her approach. She cupped his nose in her hands and kissed him. Swiftly she slipped a bridle over his head then led him out over a grass verge. At the paddock she hitched up her voluminous chemise over her pantalettes, tossed back a woollen cape and, grasping Jet's mane, swung on to his back.

Shunning bridle paths, she made for the high meadows of Chadlett Hill and the South Downs. At the crest of the hill she slowed to a walk and looked for the gypsy encampment in the mist of the valley. Ghostly shapes of gypsy horses grazing the lower swards were all she could discern. She had hoped to see Gorran on his piebald pony starting out to join her, but all was quiet. Her jaunt that morning would be without the gypsy boy.

She turned Jet to continue her ride. Gathering speed she came into full gallop, fearlessly clearing hedges, ditches and fences. Her hair which had been bound in a silk turban now flowed over her shoulders, and her chemise, torn and soiled by hedgerow brambles, billowed as wings at her back.

She knew Jet shared the exhilaration of these secret dawn excursions. There was exultation in their performance, away from the prying eyes of her tutor and his wife. They would term it a misdemeanour to ride with such abandon without benefit of correct habit or side-saddle. It was a gesture of defiance and means of escape from the monotony of her life.

The sun, now risen, shone on steaming fields as she slowed to a canter. She had been out for over an hour. Suddenly, a bright flash on the far hill caused her to rein in. She shaded her eyes with both hands to see the source of the flashing light. There it was again. It was coming from Chadlett Copse. She lowered her hands. Again the flash. At the edge of trees she saw a patch of white, then a movement. With a gasp she recognized one of the massive grey horses from Adversane House. Another flash. The gentleman mounted on the grey was holding a field glass to his eye, and the sun caught the lens again.

Was she being watched? The thought disturbed her. She was anxious that only

Gorran knew of these dawn rides for, if widely known, the mode of her riding would brand her a person of impropriety. She could not risk that, for her father's sake. She must return to the manor house with all speed and be a-bed before anyone stirred. Grasping the reins she urged Jet forward, lying low along his back until out of sight of Chadlett Copse.

In a meadow below the home farm, she dismounted and led Jet back to his stable, where she removed the bridle. Her hands shook as she tended and rugged him, then she crept across the yard and into the house.

She paused at the staircase, startled by sounds of unusual activity in the kitchen and serveries. A footman and housemaid were setting the table in the formal dining-room, and the smell of frying bacon and braising kidneys confirmed an important breakfast in preparation. No one saw her as she quickly mounted the stairs and slipped into her room.

For a moment she stood with her back to the door, breathing heavily and hushing the two dalmatians that leapt to greet her.

'Gus, Gussie, good dogs. Quiet now. Lie down.'

They followed her as she threw off her cape and hid her torn chemise under the mattress before donning another. From a drawer she took a lace cap, placed it on her head and settled back into bed. Gus and Gussie lay beside her on an old red velvet powdering-robe they had adopted.

Was the rider at Chadlett Copse on his way to the manor house? If so, he could be her new guardian, the young Earl of Adversane. Her tutor, the Reverend Lachbone, had pointed him out as heir and successor at the funeral of the old earl. She had been so heavily veiled that she could hardly see anything on that sad day, least of all the deportment and visage of the new earl. Was she to meet him now? Unlikely, she thought, for she had not been invited to the breakfast about to be served downstairs. Her breathing and heartbeat calmed. She closed her eyes and drowsed.

A rapping on the door awoke her with a start. She delayed a response until she heard the urgent request of Nell, her maid.

'Miss Sophie, may I come in?'

'Of course, Nell,' said Sophie, sitting up.

Nell entered and opened the casement curtains, drew back the bed drapes and drove out the dogs. Sophie saw that she was flushed and agitated.

'What's afoot, Nell, that makes you ill-disposed this morning?'

'I've had to wait at table besides my other work. That Mr Hynde Hallam arrived from Adversane, invited to breakfast by the Reverend and Mrs Lachbone to welcome the new earl to the manor house. Ordering us all about . . .'

'Did the earl come with him?'

'No. He came later, mounted on his own horse.'

The rider on the hill, thought Sophie.

Nell placed clean drying-cloths in the wash-closet and poured hot water from a brass ewer into a bowl.

'Why was I not invited to take breakfast with them?'

Nell drew a blue-silk morning-gown from the wardrobe.

'The meal is nigh finished, Miss Sophie. I was surprised not to see you at the table. The young earl has asked to meet you, and the Lachbones had no option but to instruct me to make sure you came down soonest.'

'So the Lachbones knew about a guest for breakfast this morning but didn't think to tell me.'

'It would seem so, Miss Sophie.'

'I wonder why old Lachbone didn't invite me. So that they could convey some bad reports, Nell?'

Nell nodded, then came close to Sophie. Lowering her voice, she said:

'I'm not one for tale-telling, but the Lachbones and that Mr Hallam from Adversane were full of complaints. They said you're an inattentive pupil, difficult to teach, and . . .' she hesitated.

'Go on, Nell. What else do they think of me?'

'That you're dilatory, lazy and a lie-abed!'

Sophie smiled. She was not in the habit of exchanging gossip with staff but, angry at her exclusion, she knew that Nell shared her sentiments.

'They say these things to justify their continued employment in the hope of my improvement,' Sophie mused.

'That's their game, no doubt about it!'

Sophie scrambled out of bed. 'Then I'll play a game of my own! I shall demonstrate how useless their efforts have been. Nell, leave me for a moment. Tell them I have just awoken and shall prepare myself to join them.'

Nell smiled. 'I'll be back to take you down.'

If the Lachbones reported that she was a lazy lie-abed, Sophie was willing to prove it this morning in a ruse to hide her identity from the rider of the grey.

She discarded the silk morning-gown and, after shaking off the looser dogs' hairs, slipped into the old and creased red velvet powdering-robe. Her hand-mirror showed rosy cheeks from the morning ride so she dashed blanching powder over her face. She grimaced at the pallor that resulted, which made her blue eyes sink into dark circles.

Not a wisp of hair was allowed to escape her lace cap, and she tucked in a few curling rags to frame her face. As a final touch, she placed shapeless felt slippers over her feet. 'To prove a point,' she said to herself.

A tap on the door announced Nell's return.

19

Sophie opened the door and stood on the threshold. Nell cupped a hand to her mouth, agape at the spectacle before her.

'Miss Sophie, what are you about!'

Sophie placed a forefinger on her lips. 'I'm ready to go down now, Nell.'

Nell preceded her and opened the door to the dining-room. Sophie slowly followed and stared at the three persons still seated at the table. Conversation ceased abruptly. Scandalized looks froze on the faces of Mrs Lachbone and Mr Hallam.

After a knowing glance at his wife, the Reverend Lachbone rose and approached. His lips shone with grease from the breakfast fare.

'My dear Miss Stapleford. I see we have disturbed your slumbers. But for a very good reason.'

Sophie made no comment. She wondered why the earl was not at the table.

'Indeed, a very good reason,' added Mrs Lachbone.

Then the sallow-faced Mr Hallam said: 'The Lord Adversane is here to make your acquaintance. He has stepped into the breach as your guardian. You should be very grateful to him.'

There was a movement from the window to her left, as a tall elegant young gentleman confronted her. He made a stiff bow.

'Miss Sophia Stapleford,' he said. 'It is an honour to serve you.'

She was struck dumb. His impeccable riding-habit fitted without a wrinkle and a black fob-ribbon depended from his pocket. Other mourning touches featured his black stock and shining top boots over doeskin breeches. His rich brown hair was clipped short. As he regarded her, she noticed fine dark eyebrows gathered in a frown and reproach in his grey eyes.

He turned and ushered her to a fireside chair, then stood with his back to the mantel. She looked up, but was met by an expression of cold indifference as he stared ahead.

'I am sorry your welfare has been neglected during my father's long illness, but I am determined to put the matter to rights,' he said punctiliously.

'Oh,' she replied, 'I did not think myself neglected at all, and had great sympathy for your father's suffering. Please do not impose so severe an obligation on yourself.'

He lowered his gaze and for some moments appeared to be studying the Turkish hearth-rug. Then, in a softer tone he added:

'Nevertheless, Miss Stapleford, I feel matters should remain as they are for the moment, but I shall return to review the entire circumstance of your welfare under the terms of the guardianship.'

She nodded assent despite a surge of disappointment that it seemed the *status quo* would continue. She stole a glance at the table where the others were chatting together. Quietly, she asked:

'Have you heard news of my father of late?'

'Alas, no. I shall lodge enquiries with friends I have at the Admiralty and will write to your father advising him of the changed situation in your case.'

There was a silence as she blinked back tears.

He suddenly stooped and levelled his eyes to her. In a hushed voice, he said:

'Remember, I'm your guardian and in place of your father until he returns. You must trust me and tell me if I need to do anything to further your wellbeing.'

'There's a long list,' she whispered.

'You must trust me,' he repeated as he stood up.

She nodded imperceptibly, biting her lip.

'It's a fine day for early calls and early rides,' he remarked briskly to the company at large. 'Few were about this morning. Do you ever take early rides, Miss Stapleford? My head groom, Mr Seb Broadrib, tells me you are a living lesson in equestrian skills when mounted.'

Sophie was alarmed by his reference to early rides.

'I much prefer driving,' she said, to change the subject.

'I hear you're greatly adept with the ribbons, too.'

'I would not so claim, my lord. Enjoyment of all participants is the criterion, with knowledge of the equipage and mastery of the horses achieved by understanding and affection.'

'An admirable approach, Miss Stapleford, in line with my own.'

She was pleased at the earl's response, but the rasping voice of Mr Hallam interposed.

'There's still the matter of the gypsies, my lord.'

His comment clouded her optimism. What could he mean?

'Ah, yes,' added the Reverend Lachbone. 'You must direct that their camp be demolished. You are new to country ways, my lord, and to harbour gypsies at Adversane invites trouble. They practise mysterious rites, commit felonies and when caught can vanish like quicksilver.'

'I'm not disposed to discuss the matter at the moment,' said the earl. 'The gypsies are employed to crop the copses. They are not here the entire year. All the Acts against them were repealed by King George, and no authority may move them after sundown wherever they are.'

'There are ways round such stipulations,' rejoined Hallam.

The earl did not comment but Sophie saw that he gave Hallam a dubious look. She must warn the gypsies at the first opportunity.

The earl made preparations to withdraw, bowing to the ladies and shaking the hands of the gentlemen. She saw his tall figure framed in the doorway, attended by a footman. He was leaving, and she had so many things to say. The words they had exchanged did not come near the reassurance she desired. She followed him to the porch, where a groom stood with his grey.

She tried to moderate the desperation she felt as she addressed him.

'My lord, I look to you for immediate change in my circumstances. I long for something to happen, but my days are spent with the very old who cannot understand my needs and desires. I am unhappy in their company and am harshly judged. Please help me, or I shall be forced to . . .'

'You shall be forced to do what, Miss Stapleford?' he asked quietly, pulling on his gloves.

'Run away with the gypsies!' she said in a rush.

He regarded her. 'You would fit in with them very well, I should think.'

She puffed, pouted and fumed, suddenly ashamed of her unkempt appearance. She had sought to discredit the Lachbones by dressing so, but had simply disgraced herself in the eyes of her guardian. Her cheeks burned.

'I am not blind to facts, Miss Stapleford,' he continued. 'There had to be a reason for your behaviour, and I am now aware of it. I assure you there will be changes, so don't feel you have to join the gypsies.'

He turned and mounted the grey with an ease she admired. He looked down at her. 'When you ride like the wind at the break of day, are you in pursuit of something?'

She gulped as joy flooded. He had kept her secret. She whipped off her cap and shook free her fair curls. There was no need for pretence now.

'You have not answered my question, Miss Stapleford,' he pressed. 'What is the object of the chase?'

'Dreams!' she cried defiantly.

'Insubstantial as a quarry, in my opinion,' said he, tipping his hat as he rode away.

CHAPTER TWO

Guy was deep in thought as he left the manor house, confused after meeting Miss Stapleford. He had looked at the word *guardian* in a dictionary, hoping for some enlightenment in such a role. Its meanings of *guard* and *protect* were broad, not specific for his purpose. It was obvious the tutors were at fault in permitting Miss Stapleford to present herself in such a way. Or should it fall to him as her guardian to correct or instruct? He did not know what to think or how to act.

His *émigré* friend, Anton, had laughed when Guy told him about his inherited ward. '*Tiens!* Marry her to a footman, Guy, and finish with it,' he suggested. Would any footman want her? As Sir Henry had warned, she was in conflict with the expectations of society.

He had noted her distress at the mention of her father, and thought it pitiful that her mother, Lady May Stapleford, had met an untimely death. She had been hailed as the most refined beauty of her generation. Yet her daughter possessed few feminine graces; but spirit in abundance, he had to admit. He recalled the rider, splendid in the dawn light, and the clownlike pallor of her face looking up at him. The dazzlingly lovely hair suddenly released from the shabby cap, and her response to his questions, had momentarily taken his breath away.

'Whoa, Japhet!' he exclaimed as his grey stumbled. The path through the copse had narrowed into a stony gully, making it necessary to concentrate on guiding his mount to an area where the trees thinned at the high point of Chadlett Hill. He reined in and dismounted. Reassuring himself that Japhet had sustained no injury from his stumbling, he took out his field glass and looked down into the valley. From this vantage point he could see Adversane House, set down solid and stately amid its vast park and estate. He welcomed this feature of his inheritance, but he was incommoded at the prospect of guiding and protecting Miss Stapleford.

On the valley floor, his gaze followed the meandering gleam of the river. Some six miles upriver his elder sister, the Lady Elizabeth Dallimore, lived with her charming family. 'My dear and precious Beth,' he murmured. The upper reaches were still swathed in mist, which was dispersing as he watched, revealing the river's verdant course. Now his next move was clear. He closed the field glass, thrust it into its case, remounted Japhet and set off briskly for home. A chat with sister Beth might well provide a solution to his great quandary.

*   *   *

Since Sophie had met her new guardian, time hung heavily as she was longing to hear of his plans for her. As the days went by she drifted along with the monotonous routines imposed by her tutors.

The captain's room of the manor house became her retreat. She sat at his desk, tidying the quills and topping up the inkwells in readiness for his longed-for return. This was where she wrote her pieces of prose and poems, placing them in a leather-covered box to await her father's scrutiny. She opened the box, inspected the contents and, in closing it, marvelled that she had not put pen to paper

27

for many weeks. The old earl's death had affected her greatly, particularly since her visits to him had been curtailed by Hallam on the grounds of the earl's worsening health. She resented this, especially since Hallam had dismissed Mr and Mrs Parker, the earl's butler and head housekeeper. There was no one to whom she could appeal, for all the loyal retainers had also been discharged.

Sighing, she left the desk and raised the cover of the spinet, recalling the musical interludes she had shared with her father. The tidy untouched state of the sheet music emphasized the cessation of this pastime since his capture. This morning, she sat gloomily wondering when Hallam would leave the manor house.

He had unexpectedly dallied for two days since the earl's visit, closeted with the Lachbones in their apartment and emerging only for long walks with them in the park, heads together in close converse. Sophie knew that the surprising decision of the young earl to live permanently at Adversane had caused a stir, and it was clear that they thought he would soon tire of the country and return to London. His presence threatened the authority enjoyed by Hallam during the prolonged illness of the old earl. Sophie guessed that high on their agenda was a plot to remove the gypsies.

Though anxious to warn Gorran, she was

loath to leave the manor house until Hallam returned to Adversane. The Lachbones raised no questions about her driving excursions but, given the opportunity, Hallam was wont to spy upon her.

The door opened to admit a breathless Nell.

'Look from the window, Miss Sophie,' she whispered, 'and you'll see the going of Mr Hallam.'

Sophie rushed to the window. By the porch the Lachbones were bidding farewell to Hallam, who was seated with a driver in his black curricle.

'Good,' said Sophie, turning away. 'Nell, I'd like you to go to the carriage house and ask one of the grooms to prepare the gig and hackney for my use this afternoon.'

'Shall you take luncheon before you go?'

'No. Best that I report to Mrs Lachbone now she is free.'

Later that morning, after a tedious sewing-session with Mrs Lachbone, Sophie took a light refreshment before she changed into her driving dress. She walked across to the carriage house, tying a pale-blue veil around her low-crowned hat. The gig and hackney stood ready. A groom assisted her entry and soon she was away, calling the dalmatians to pace beside her.

She drove towards Chadlett Hill, then chose a tree-lined decline where the tracery of branches splintered the sunlight. As the lane levelled, she increased speed expecting that Gus and Gussie would soon be challenged by gypsy dogs. All was quiet and the campsite deserted. Gorran's *vardo* had gone, the gypsies had moved away.

With mixed feelings of sadness and relief, Sophie continued down the lane, then turned the gig on an open common and made her way back to the site. By a dark copse of larch and holly, Gus suddenly bounded ahead and with yelps of joy greeted Gorran as he stepped into the lane. Sophie halted as he took hold of the horse's harness, producing from his pocket a carrot which the horse munched with satisfaction.

This child, thought Sophie as she regarded him, could confer vitality to any sluggard mount by some innate genius of the ancient horse-peoples of Europe. He had the wiry physique of a boy of eight for all his eleven years and was brown as a ripe mayberry, his bright black eyes taking account of everything. She noted he was puzzled by her appearance at the camp. A frown intruded after his grin of welcome.

'I wanted to see you on an urgent matter,' said Sophie.

'What's toward, then?'

'I overheard the Reverend Lachbone and Mr Hallam trying to persuade Lord Adversane to demolish your camp. I see you have moved on, and I hope it was not prompted by any threat or action on their part.'

Gorran shook his head. 'My uncle decided we should go. He sees and hears many things while working on the estate, and we did not wish to cause trouble for the new earl. We're going to earth like the dog-fox. Thank you for your warning, my *rawnie.*'

'When shall you leave, Gorran?'

'As soon as my uncle returns with my pony, who was put to harness to help in the move. Are you going back to the manor house?'

'Yes, now that I am satisfied you have moved away of your own volition.'

'I'll ride with you for a while,' he said, climbing up beside her.

She started off at a walk and they drove in silence until she asked: 'Where will you go?'

'Best that you know nothing, but you can think on it.'

'I have to know something to think on it.'

'You know the country markets and the horse fairs. Somewhere about these places we shall be. When we know it is safe, we shall come back to Adversane.'

'How will you know?'

'By reading the hedgerows and roadsides. We leave signals in ways you would not dream of. These are called in our language *patrins*. We shall know, never fear.'

She drove on until the woodland gave way to open fields, then drew to a stop.

'So it's farewell for a while, my young friend.

You know where I am if you want help in any way.'

Gorran jumped down. He plucked a newly sprouted twig from a nearby creeper and, handing it to her, said:

'Traveller's Joy, or what you will. When this silvers the hedgerows, we shall return.'

Sophie placed the twig in her pocket. Gorran lightly spanked the flank of the hackney and she continued on her way. Looking back, she saw his slight figure standing in the lane. The next time she looked, he had gone.

Gorran was the only friend she had outside Adversane. Sometimes on her rides she had seen carriages pass, full of fashionable young ladies on their way to one of the grand houses in the area. She envied their gaiety and friendship; somehow she was excluded from such gatherings. Once, at an Adversane House function before the death of the old earl, she saw a young gentleman leap on to a moving phaeton and present a nosegay to the lady occupant before tenderly embracing her. Every time she envisaged this, voluptuous thoughts swarmed like timid sparrows and, in her musings, she cast herself as the lady in the phaeton. But the gallant beau was obscure and tarried in the shadows of her reverie. Now that the young earl had entered her consciousness, she felt this lack in her life more keenly, but could not presume she occupied the minutest part of his thoughts.

A lowness of spirit came upon her as she drove back. The sun had lost its strength and the incline slowed the pace. The tree-tunnels now appeared gloomy and threatening. Even the dogs had raced ahead and were out of sight.

She entered the yard and led the hackney to the waiting groom.

'A good drive,' she said to him. In her heart she did not think it was a good drive at all.

The next morning, Sophie was in the captain's room determined to start a poem, when Mrs Lachbone approached her.

'I must tell you that we have received a note from Adversane House. The Lord Adversane and his sister, Lady Elizabeth Dallimore, are coming to call in a se'nnight to take tea with us.'

Sophie started. 'Oh. With the Lady Elizabeth?'

'Yes,' said Mrs Lachbone darkly. 'There are some changes to come.'

'Oh,' said Sophie again.

It's happening, she thought. I have been waiting for something to happen, and now it is. She put down her pen, unable to write further, her mind in a flurry.

Sleep eluded her that night. A tea-party at the manor house! It was unheard of. Frantic doubts displaced her excitement at the prospect. Mrs Lachbone had entertained one or two ladies from the village for tea in her apartment, but this demanded a different approach.

She rose quickly and completed her toilette. She felt sure the earl and his sister were coming in answer to her plea for change. 'It is on my account,' she murmured, brushing her hair vigorously, 'and I shall take charge of the affair. Changes are overdue here, too.' She gathered her hair and pinned it back with two sapphire-topped gold pins that had belonged to her mother. 'There!' she said softly, regarding herself. 'I shall be hostess and will suffer no more exclusion from social events in my father's house!' She was determined to be party to all arrangements and would no longer confine herself to the shadows. Her duty was plain, she would take her place.

She turned and, followed by Gus and Gussie, entered the salon to take breakfast there instead of being served in her room. The staff hastily set a place for her and waited for instructions.

'Please release the dogs and then bring me tea, wheaten rolls and cook's currant conserve,' she said, 'and afterwards I wish to see Nell in my room.'

While waiting to be served, she looked around the salon. The dinginess of winter lurked everywhere. Spring was advancing. The heavy curtains should have been changed and the windows cleaned. She would consult with the housekeeper to make sure that the furniture and all appurtenances were sparkling and worthy to be seen by the important guests who were coming to tea. She was taut with energy and eagerness to transform the management of the manor house. She smiled, drumming her fingers on the table, for she had taken a pigeon-step in the direction of transforming herself.

CHAPTER THREE

Adversane House

Guy was possessed by an exuberant sense of purpose since visiting his sister at Rothervale House. She had returned with him yesterday, and now he waited for her to refine plans before their proposed visit to the manor house.

He chose to manage the house and estate from an octagon room abutting the library. It was here that Guy set up his office with a pleasant sitting-room, which enjoyed unimpeded views across the terrace and gardens. There was constant light within, diffused through muslin under-curtains as the sun traversed its course, enlivening the rich sheen of eight Chinese-silk panels on the walls.

Guy rose from his desk, and tidied the

estate documents he had been studying. He looked up as, after a light tap on the door, the Lady Elizabeth entered, followed by a footman with a tray.

'A little respite for you, Guy. Fruit-wine and pound-cake,' she said as the footman placed the tray upon a table by the chimney-piece.

'Thank you.' Guy smiled, dismissing the footman and ushering his sister to a chair. 'I'm happy for the diversion. One can have too much of rods and perches.'

He poured the drink into two glasses, then joined her after first pinning back a muslin curtain at the window to reveal the garden better. They sipped their wine in the silence of mutual ease, enjoying the expanse of sunlit lawn with islands of shrubs amid dark angles of cedars.

'I'm so pleased you were able to come, Beth,' said Guy softly.

She smiled. 'Toby expects to be at home for weeks until the madness of Westminster settles down. Thus I am released.'

'How strange it is that far-removed major tragedies touch our ordinary lives. Poor Perceval, to be so unmercifully gunned down! Who does Sir Toby think will follow him?'

'All is in flux depending upon the Prince Regent. Toby thinks our next Prime Minister will be Lord Liverpool.'

'A high Tory. How does Sir Toby Dallimore MP view that?'

'To be a Tory in a Whig government is good, and to be a Whig in a Tory government is better; but to be an Independent is best of all—and an Independent he prefers to remain. At this moment . . .'

'Yes?'

'The parliamentary gentleman is building a pigsty!'

Guy smiled as he offered pieces of pound-cake. 'Like Farmer George, I see that Sir Toby shares delight in rural life.'

'He is never happier than when at Rothervale,' she said, 'and has learned the art of surveying to an almost professional standard. His plans for improvement are impressive and, to my mind, ambitious; but his enthusiasm overflows and drowns my caution.'

Guy rose, refilled his glass and stood by the window in silence for some moments. Then he turned to face her.

'Beth, I don't know how to tell you this, it's a matter I'm reluctant to raise; but our dear father was relentlessly exploited over the years he suffered in sickness. This has resulted in our inheritance being subject to the importunities of creditors and duns to an alarming degree.'

'But it should not be!' she exclaimed. 'Toby has told me that the sales of lumber and gravel from this estate have been prodigious. His coach has been constantly held up by dawdling overloaded wagons from Adversane. He thought father highly enriched by such commercial exploits.'

'Someone was, but not our father.'

She drew breath. 'Then who . . . ?'

In answer he placed his right index finger to his lips, went quickly to the door and opened it, advancing a step into the corridor. He looked to the right and left, then returned, closing the door softly behind him. By that time Beth had risen as if to follow him, a frown furrowing her brow.

'Do not be alarmed, Beth. I had to make sure we would not be interrupted. There's much to impart but for your ears only.'

'What is amiss, then?'

'Sir Henry Nancarrow, who continues to manage all our properties, warned me of something irregular going on here. It hasn't taken me long to find out what it is. Forests have been felled and the lumber sold but the estate has not gained a penny from such sales. Also, the land has been quarried for a certain type of gravel needed by roadmakers such as Telford, and again not a ha'penny to our credit.'

'Who is responsible for this?'

'I think it's father's steward, Hynde Hallam, but I don't wish him to know of my suspicions. Hallam and his associates are waiting for me to take up my London life again and are lying low. Why father engaged that man is a mystery.'

'What will you do?'

'I'm trying to arrive at a figure to lodge a claim against Hallam but I have not yet explored the far reaches of the estate where these unauthorized activities have occurred. I need a professional to inspect the entire area with me and calculate damage. Hallam blames the gypsies.' He laughed. 'I've had to play the role of a complete booby in these matters, Beth, to make them think I have neither interest nor desire to manage the estate. Hallam thinks that I should sell all the land except the garden.'

Beth was silent, her head bowed. After some moments she looked up, engaging him fully.

'What more natural consequence would it be for you to explore your inherited lands in company with your brother-in-law?'

'With Sir Toby?'

'He is unknown to Hallam, and would be regarded simply as a member of the family paying a visit. Your excursions with him would raise no curiosity, yet he is expert in the aspects of land assessment you need. You must engage Toby at once!'

Guy's heart raced. It could be the answer. He turned to regard her. Her head was still tilted in concern, but her bright countenance belied the sobriety of her dove-grey mourning-dress and unadorned lace cap.

'Beth,' he said softly, 'I am already indebted

to you for your offer to bestow Miss Stapleford. It is too much to expect both Dallimores to be involved in solutions to my inheritance worries.'

'Nonsense!' she cried. 'Toby must stay as your guest at Adversane, and I will arrange it as soon as I return.'

'But—' he began.

'Enough, Guy,' she said, raising her hands with palms turned outward. 'As a family we must stand against such charlatans. That is my final comment. Now let us turn to the more pleasant subject of Miss Stapleford.'

He sighed. 'I suppose we must.'

'I met her but once with the captain. I remember a mischievous little five-year-old with a wealth of golden hair.'

'That description could easily apply but with the dubious maturity granted by some fourteen extra years.'

'Guy, you are grudging in your talk of her. I feel sympathy for her plight. Father obviously took his duties seriously until his illness, and now it remains for us to make good the neglect of her wellbeing and development. The twins are so looking forward to her joining us.'

'I hope they'll not find her dull company. She seems remarkably untalented, except in equestrian matters, and resents tutoring in intellectual pursuits.'

'Perhaps her tutors are unsuitable and fail to engage her.'

He shrugged. 'Who knows? They complain of a rebellious nature, locking herself in her father's room and taking studying time there amid his books.'

'I presume they think the captain's books inappropriate?'

'The tutors feel they may negate their instruction on moral standards.'

Beth smiled, shaking her head.

Guy continued: 'You do realize you will also be burdened with Nell, a personal maid, a gig and hackney, a black gelding called Jet, and two dalmatians, Gus and Gussie . . .'

Beth nodded. 'Seriously, though, have you managed to find a place for the Lachbones?'

'There may be a school appointment for both in Somerset.'

'Good. And is it possible to inform the captain of these new arrangements for his daughter?'

'That is in hand. I have a contact at the Admiralty. The last they heard was that the captain is held in a chateau somewhere in Artois, but is moved frequently. He is of high rank and of value to his captors. They may be holding him to bargain for the release of a French prisoner of comparable rank.'

'How do they know these things?'

'A web of spies, Beth.'

There was a long silence. Then Beth spoke.

'As to Miss Stapleford's prospects, we shall have to ignore this London season, but we can plan for next year. Perhaps we may justify a late appearance by saying she has been living deep in the country with continuous maladies of a infectious nature, and connections with a family in mourning. After all, she is nineteen.'

'Does that matter?' he asked.

'Of course. There would be no need to consider a London season if, in the meantime, she marries well.'

'There's little chance of that.'

'Remember, she has the potential to become a beauty like her mother.'

'We shall have to see if she improves under your care,' he said guardedly, moving to the window where he remained staring at the garden. So this is all I would retain, he thought, if Hallam had his wish. Beyond the trees and manicured lawns stretched the verdant miles of meadows and woodlands, precious to his inheritance. His jaw clenched. He will never surrender Adversane, and Hallam and his cronies shall learn that the seventh Earl will fight to its last grain of earth. He reached to unpin the muslin curtain which fell into its place.

Beth gazed at him, a smile playing on her lips. He was handsome, elegant in the country style. How well he was suited to be a figure in that landscape! Would he harmonize with it and remain at Adversane? She wondered whether his London life and connections would persuade him otherwise. There had

been many young ladies of the *ton* who had
been linked with him from time to time; but no
serious dalliance had yet come to her ear. With
no attachments to divert his plans, Guy could
well establish himself at Adversane fulfilling,
thought Beth, their father's last whispered
wish.

The Manor House

Sophie pensively inspected the contents of
her wardrobe. There seemed to be a
preponderance of dark riding- and driving-
wear, apart from one blue-silk morning-gown.
She owned no formal afternoon- or evening-
gowns at all. Symbolic of my life, she thought.

Turning away, she wondered how she could
possibly entertain to tea the young earl and his
sister in the only silk gown she possessed. She
wished to associate herself with their family
period of mourning, and the bright blue colour
was not appropriate. A darker hue, even a
grey, would be more suited to the occasion.

Suddenly, she summoned Nell.

'Bring candles to the lumber-room, Nell.
There is a chest there in which some of my
mother's dresses have been stored. They are
probably in the style of some twenty years
since, but the stuff must be of the finest. Let us
see what is there.'

Nell quickly gathered up a candle-branch,

and Sophie followed her up a flight of stairs and along a panelled passage to the far end of the house. Picking their way through much disorder, together they drew out the chest and threw back its lid. Under layers of calico, covered with dried rose petals, several dresses had been carefully folded.

'I see my father's loving hand in this,' Sophie whispered. 'It's as if he expected her to return.'

'She *has* returned in you, Miss Sophie. All say you resemble that beautiful lady, your mother,' said Nell. There was a silence as they stared into the chest, reluctant to disturb its contents. Sophie blinked back a sudden moistness in her eyes, then said briskly:

'Let us simply remove one of sober hue which would be suitable for me to wear when the earl and Lady Elizabeth call upon us.' She paused. 'It will require much alteration.'

Nell flushed with enthusiasm. 'Tomorrow I will ask Dilly Broadrib to visit us,' she said. 'She's a natural sempstress and makes Seb's and Jem's shirts an' all. She could sew a fine gown for you.'

Meanwhile Sophie had uncovered a dress of sheer French cambric made with a train. It was finely striped in white and lavender which gave an overall impression of blue-grey.

'This will suffice,' said Sophie breathlessly. 'Take the dress and hang it carefully in my room, Nell. Ask Dilly to come tomorrow with her needles and shears. Time is short and there's much to do.'

'I will, Miss Sophie,' said Nell, swept along with the excitement of her mistress.

Nell withdrew, bearing the dress as if it were a newborn, while Sophie stood by the door and glanced back into the lumber-room. She must order that it be tidied, at least for ease of access.

Since taking a more active part in management of the house, she had found the staff eager to carry out her bidding. Spring flowers decked the tables and the displayed silver and plate sparkled. Cream silk and chenille-fringed draperies had replaced the dark curtains, admitting a lightness in atmosphere and ambience.

The Lachbones suddenly became 'indisposed' and confined themselves to their apartment. When Sophie came upon Mrs Lachbone, that lady fluttered and flitted like a feather in a draught. Sophie could understand their anxieties about the future, and guessed the added tension was not unrelated to the now frequent visits of Hynde Hallam. What is it that binds this unlikely trio, she wondered.

The captain's room served as Dilly's workplace for the renovation of Lady May's dress, assisted by Nell. They had applied themselves daily to this task, and the day before the tea-party Sophie was summoned for a final fitting.

Dilly's nimble hands and knowing eye had discovered a gown within a gown. The long train had vanished, the waist raised higher and the back tailored to ensure the fashionable vertical line. Old lace trimmed the neckline and wrists, and bows were attached to Sophie's kid shoes. The colour mounted in Sophie's cheeks as she observed Dilly's and Nell's excited response to the fitting. Dilly cleared her workplace of all but her shears, and made a motion to Nell.

'Miss Sophie,' said Nell, 'would you permit Dilly to shorten your hair? She has made a cockade and fillet for a new fashion.'

'Shorten my hair?'

'Yes,' said Dilly firmly. 'If 'tis cut 'twill curl over your head and this'—she indicated the fillet—'will contain it. The cockade should be placed above your left eye.'

Sophie pondered. 'I have never worn short hair.'

'Chaperons and modistes in London houses gossip, and when ladies' maids return to the country we learn of their mistresses' fashions. For a young girl, the short curly style is in vogue,' said Dilly.

'Then cut it,' said Sophie, without hesitation.

When Dilly's shears ceased snipping, Nell placed the band over the golden curls and arranged the cockade. Sophie, looking in the cheval-glass for the first time, gasped with delight at the astonishing change in her appearance.

She circled, regarding herself from every angle.

'Unbelievable,' she breathed. 'Dilly and Nell, your talents are remarkable. Now I shall enjoy the tea-party.'

She hugged Dilly who, tut-tutting at the show of gratitude, withdrew with Nell, smiling and satisfied with their handiwork.

Later that day, Sophie was seated at her father's desk when somewhere upstairs a door slammed violently, echoing throughout the house. Moments later she was startled as the main front door closed with a boom. Through a window she saw Mrs Lachbone walking quickly towards the summerhouse, a favourite retreat, her hands grappling with errant ribbons to secure her straw bonnet from a stiffening evening breeze.

Sophie had been trying to gain Mrs Lachbone's ear whenever she glimpsed her alone in the kitchen or still room. Mrs Lachbone usually scuttled off with a loaded tray in haste to avoid contact. Seldom unaccompanied by her husband, her lone appearance in the garden provided an opportunity Sophie could not ignore, despite Mrs Lachbone's slamming of doors and hurried departure from the house. It was plain that something had put her out of countenance; but Sophie decided to persist, since there was an omission on her part that she wished to put right.

The coming visit of the earl and his sister was significant.

Change was in the air and no one dared to speculate as to the course it would take. Sophie felt sure the Lachbones would be moving on from the manor house, and hoped they would be replaced by someone younger and more amenable. Of late, she had felt sympathy for Mrs Lachbone with whom she had had the most contact, and had admired her artistic talents. Above all she acknowledged her enduring patience with a demanding, indolent and ill-tempered Reverend Lachbone. Sophie was anxious for Mrs Lachbone to take part in the tea-party alongside herself, and her husband must also be persuaded to join the social occasion. It was to make sure of this that she sought Mrs Lachbone.

Sophie left the desk and went up to her room. After a pause to admire again the dress she was to wear the next day, she draped a shawl around her shoulders, went into the garden and calmly but purposefully approached the summerhouse.

At the edge of the garden, the summerhouse turned its back on the formal lawns and faced a thicket bordering a copse, beyond which lay the undulating parklands of Adversane. One large room extended to a veranda where stood a curved wooden bench. There Mrs Lachbone sat, darkly cloaked and stiff as a ramrod, the only movement her fingers nervously picking a white kerchief lodged in her lap.

Sophie did not wish to alarm Mrs Lachbone, and trod heavily on the path to warn of her arrival. Mrs Lachbone maintained her composure, raising watery and red-rimmed eyes as Sophie seated herself beside her.

'I have been anxious to talk with you, Mrs Lachbone,' she said softly, 'and hope this intrusion is not untimely.' Mrs Lachbone shuddered as if cold, as Sophie continued: 'You are distressed. Please let me help.'

'That is kind. But there is little you can do.' Mrs Lachbone paused, then took a deep breath, nodding her head several times which set her bonnet ribbons rustling. 'I continue to have grave disagreements with my husband . . .' Another pause followed. Then she faced Sophie. 'He, that is my husband, seems incapable of rebuffing a certain person's interference in my—or rather our—affairs. Now we are on the point of leaving the manor house and Lord Adversane's service, that person's demands are becoming intolerable.' She raised the kerchief to mask her face as a silence ensued.

Sophie was taken aback by this unexpected turn in the conversation. The 'certain person' must surely be Hynde Hallam, she thought.

'If you expect to be leaving the locality, then a new start in a new place may present an escape from this person,' Sophie suggested.

Mrs Lachbone lowered the kerchief and placed a hand on Sophie's arm.

'I pray that will happen.'

'I'm certain it will, and perhaps soon.'

'Nevertheless, I shall be sad to leave Adversane. My father was rector to the fifth Earl. My childhood was spent here, followed by my time as a young wife married to the dear man who took over the curacy and served with my father. The idyll was swiftly shattered. Within five years, I had lost my parents and my husband. I became a "relict". Isn't that a horrid word? As a relict of one clergyman, I married another, Clarence Lachbone.'

Sophie sighed, saddened that exchanges on this personal level had somehow evaded them over the years.

'I did not realize you had prior connections with Adversane,' she whispered.

'It was a pastoral paradise; but now . . .' Again she shuddered, her hand pressing on Sophie's arm. 'Perhaps you *can* help me.'

'I will do anything to lessen your distress.'

Mrs Lachbone rose abruptly and stood by the wooden paling of the veranda, gazing ahead.

'I have always been fascinated by landscape,' she said. 'Ever since I could hold a pencil, I have sketched and made maps of

Adversane. Years ago in a copse by an old orchard, there was a hamlet of humble cottages with the evocative name of Nether Cherry. I made many sketches of it. There was one that I coloured and framed which I took to the manor house and placed on the wall of our sitting-room. There it remained until . . .' She paused, her head lowered and the kerchief raised again.

'Yes, go on,' urged Sophie softly.

'My husband sold it—to Hynde Hallam.' She turned to face Sophie, her mouth trembling. 'When he took it from the wall, Hallam removed it from the frame, then he lit the candle on our table and dangled the picture over the flame. Soon it was engulfed in fire! He held it until only charred pieces remained. I could not believe what I had seen, my husband and I were speechless. Why would he do such a thing? He appeared to suffer no burns on his hands. He is the very devil!'

'How strange,' breathed Sophie.

'Stranger still, he asked if I had any other drawings and paintings of that part of Adversane. If so, he said he would double the price of that which he had just destroyed. I screamed "No!" as I thought my husband was on the brink of offering other work in my portfolio. Hallam said he thought I had more, and he would return until I gave him all of them.'

'Why was it Nether Cherry that interested

51

him?'

Mrs Lachbone returned to her seat. With a lowered voice, she said:

'Because Hallam demolished Nether Cherry. It no longer exists. He lopped all the trees, banished the cottagers, and has been enriching himself with commodities from the entire estate which rightly belong to the earl.'

'Are you certain, Mrs Lachbone?'

'He will never admit to it. He blames the gypsies for the plunder. I have proof of his activities in my portfolio and that is why he wishes to destroy all that is in it.'

'He took advantage of the old earl's incapacity over those years.'

'Precisely, and there will come a time when the new earl will call him to account.'

'Your drawings could aid Lord Adversane's case, Mrs Lachbone.'

'That is how you can help. I will place my portfolio in your care so that you can present it to him in due time.'

Sophie rose and stood by the veranda palings, pondering. Then she asked:

'Is the portfolio very large?'

'No, it is no more than three palms wide.'

Sophie nodded. 'Hallam's spies are everywhere. Leave your portfolio in the large chest in the lumber-room. Place it under the dresses that are stored there. Neither Hallam nor your husband would think of looking for it there. When you have left the manor house, I will take the portfolio, guard it and give it to the earl when appropriate.'

Mrs Lachbone left the bench and joined Sophie.

'I shall rest happy in the knowledge that it is safe in your hands.'

Sophie then raised the matter that had troubled her.

'I hope you will agree to stand with me to receive the earl and his sister and join me in serving tea. It was remiss of me to delay my request until now. Please forgive me. I hope, too, that your husband will attend, especially as Hallam is *not* invited.'

A faint smile crossed Mrs Lachbone's face as she answered.

'Indeed, there is much for you to forgive, but you may rely upon our presence.' She paused. 'Your short hair becomes you, Miss Sophie.'

Evening had set in, sealing the sky in purplish splendour. Sophie took Mrs Lachbone's hand.

'If our paths are not destined to cross again, I would have you know that I admire your fortitude in these unhappy events, and be assured I will do what is right. To allay suspicion of collusion between us, I suggest that we leave the summerhouse separately.'

At that moment they were stopped by a burst of magical birdsong coming from low in the thicket. A storm of notes issued from it, followed by a silence, then flaring out into a crescendo of sheer joy.

'It's a nightingale,' whispered Mrs Lachbone.

'It's a benison,' murmured Sophie, 'signifying our harmony of purpose.'

They stood entranced, hand in hand, reluctant to interrupt the nightingale's serenade. After some moments, Mrs Lachbone released Sophie's hand and quietly left the summerhouse.

Adversane House

They had refined plans for Miss Stapleford's move to Rothervale and Sir Toby's visit to Adversane, sharpening every detail until it became wearisome to speculate further.

'Come, Beth,' said Guy, 'put on your bonnet and shawl. Let us escape the house and walk the meadows. On the way back we shall call at the stable-block where you may see our latest charmer and, while there, I will order the coach for later.'

The walk was blissful. They shared delight in spring's bounty, the blackthorn scattering white spray in the hedgerows and bluebells carpeting the copses. The patchwork sky allowed sparse sunlight, and it was not long before they retraced their steps, diverting to the stable-block. Seb, the head groom, led them to the yard where his stepson, Jem, was parading a grey gelding. For some moments they watched, fascinated by the powerful frame of the horse, the elegant head, kind eye yet bold stare.

'You must admit he has grand style, Beth,' said Guy, 'and the look of the original Darley Arab.'

'He's beautiful, satin white,' said Beth. 'What is his name?'

'We call him "Brisket", my lady,' said Seb, 'and he's Jem's favourite ride.'

'I envy you, Jem,' smiled Beth. 'You have some good gallops nearby.'

Jem grinned. 'He's a fast 'un on 'em all, and a fearless jumper, my lady.'

After a final fussing of Brisket, Guy said, 'We must go back for a light luncheon as we shall be dining at five, so have the coach ready for six of the clock, Seb.'

They walked along the terrace to the front of the house, where Guy was surprised to see the park gates opening to allow admittance of a small carriage drawn by a dark hackney.

'I have a visitor,' he said, frowning.

'Or possibly a guest,' observed Beth. 'See, there's a portmanteau loaded at the back.'

A footman from the house approached the carriage as a door opened and an elegant young gentleman in a dark cloak stepped out. He whipped off his hat and performed an exaggerated bow.

'*Bonjour,* Guy, *mon petit campagnard*,' he called.

Astonished, Guy gasped: 'Anton!' Then turning to Beth he explained, 'My friend and fencing-partner from London, Monseigneur Anton-Alexandre, Comte de Saint-Gabriel. Quite unexpected!'

Laughingly, Guy effected the introductions. Then he instructed the footman to take Anton's luggage to a guest apartment and direct the coachman to the carriage house.

During the luncheon that followed, served informally in the octagon room, Anton told Beth how, at thirteen years old, he had been sent to England by his parents to escape the unrest in France, leaving extensive estates in Poitiers. He was often in attendance at the house in Buckinghamshire where the Bourbon successor held court.

'And your parents? What was their fate?' asked Beth.

Anton sighed heavily. 'There is no trace.'

'You have my sincere sympathy,' Beth whispered.

In answer, Anton reached for her hand and kissed it.

A silence fell until Guy, to disperse the melancholy mood, asked Anton to impart the latest gossip from the London salons, to which he eagerly responded. As time advanced, Beth withdrew to change for dinner while Guy told Anton of the arrangements he had made with

Beth concerning Miss Stapleford.

'So you are going to surrender your ward to your sister, Guy! What a task you set her to put the little *tsigane* to rights!'

'It's necessary. Otherwise, I could never account to her father.'

'Ah, the good captain.'

'You know Sir John Stapleford?'

'Who does not know of him, that brave man, and you are right to be vigilant.' There was a silence. Then Anton continued: 'May I not come with you to meet your Miss Stapleford? You are going to tea, *n'est-ce pas?* All it needs is an extra little cup.'

Guy hesitated before answering this unexpected request, then agreed.

'Of course, why not! Be prepared to be totally unimpressed.'

'You have raised my curiosity. How can one be unimpressed by a young lady of nineteen? She must have *some* charm.'

'None that is obvious.'

Guy started as Anton suddenly jumped up from his chair with a shout, frantically searching in all his coat pockets. From one he produced a small sealed envelope and sank back with relief.

'Ah,' he said, placing the envelope under his nostrils and drawing a deep breath, 'that perfume! How have you lived without it all this time? Here, take it. I promised to hand you this billet-doux in person!'

Guy took it haltingly. He saw it was from Lady Charlotte Cotterell.

'She languishes for you,' Anton whispered.

Guy smiled as best he could to hide his discomfort. He had not given her a moment's thought since the coach ride in London. She was an acknowledged coquette and he had promised her nothing, knowing that his infatuation had declined. Truly he would have expected her to be married, or at least betrothed to someone else by now.

The door opened to Beth on the threshold.

'Dinner is ready to be served. You must hasten, Guy, for the coach is due at six.'

'I am coming too, my lady,' said Anton, rising.

'That is well,' smiled Beth.

Guy roused himself and summoned a manservant to show Anton to his apartment, and then bounded up the stairs to his own room. Lewis, his valet, had readied for him a grey-silk waistcoat and fresh muslin stock. He moved to a cheval-glass and tied the stock, glancing at Charlotte's letter on the small table where he had tossed it. Its wafting perfume sickened him, a reminder of London and his wasted days.

After a last adjustment to his black coat, he was ready to join the others for dinner. In a strange way he had been looking forward to visiting the manor house again, as if settling his ward with Beth represented an initial success in his endeavours; but the billet-doux from Charlotte had displeased him. Then he thought of Miss Stapleford and wondered what surprises that young lady might spring later at the manor house.

CHAPTER FOUR

The Adversane coach rocked its way over minor roads to the manor house. Guy, seated beside his sister, faced Anton who lounged across the opposite seat toying with the string of the window-blind. Guy eyed his elegant friend, and already regretted agreeing to his inclusion in the visit. Anton's curiosity about his ward and her father appeared to have no limit and dominated the discourse. This was not to Guy's liking; he thought it inappropriate to discuss aspects of Miss Stapleford's future, and he attempted to turn the converse to generalities. As the journey progressed, he admitted to resentment at Anton's unheralded appearance at a time when he was least inclined to entertain, and especially since he had no idea how long Anton proposed to stay.

Suddenly, he was aware of Beth addressing him.

'Anton must be puzzled by our strange habit of taking tea after dinner, Guy.'

'Oh,' he replied, relieved at the change in

subject, 'it's simply the best beverage to have at that time. Dr Johnson claims it amuses the evening, solaces the midnight and welcomes the morning. It's a smile-inducing cordial, and contributes marked informality to any occasion.'

'I am honoured to experience this height of English style,' declared Anton with a final flick of the blind string.

Silence reigned as the coach passed grazing cattle in the meadows of the home farm before entering a drive with tended lawns and flower-beds. They came to a halt where wide oaken doors stood open, from which two footmen advanced to attend them.

In her room, Sophie tried to ignore the pace of her heartbeat. With a last glance in the mirror, she took no action this time to diminish the flush mantling her cheek, noting that her eyes became bluer, more brilliant. There was no need to rehearse the imposition of a radiant welcoming countenance, for this was the gift of her hopes. She closed the door quietly and walked down the stairs to the inner hall where she stood alongside the Reverend and Mrs Lachbone, awaiting the visitors.

A footman opened the door to admit Guy, who strode forward, then halted. A sharp intake of breath preceded sheer astonishment as Sophie smilingly approached him. Was this beautiful young girl the odd 'little filly' he had met on the previous occasion! He bent over her proffered hand, and stared at her for an inordinate time so that he failed to effect proper introductions when Beth and Anton joined him. The ladies and Anton warmly introduced themselves, and Sophie completed the formalities by presenting the Lady Elizabeth to the Reverend and Mrs Lachbone.

Composing himself, Guy followed the ladies into the back drawing-room in company with Anton and the Reverend Lachbone. Seated together by the chimney-piece, he endeavoured to take a polite interest in the minutiae of formal conversation. His eyes were locked upon the surprising Miss Stapleford as she dispensed tea and titbits to the guests, treating all with infinite grace and charm.

How preferable, he thought, were shining eyes and glowing cheeks to the pasty beauties he had known in London! He took pleasure in watching her lissom form, enthralled by the exquisite symmetry of neck and bosom. These impressive endowments had not been evident under the ugly gown on their first meeting. He shifted uneasily, frowning. The comparison was so marked that he felt himself the victim of a prank. Nettled, he took refuge in affecting an air of nonchalance.

Guy finished his tea and turned to the Reverend Lachbone.

'My dear sir, would you and your lady wife accompany me and the Comte de Saint-Gabriel for a spell in the garden? Perhaps we could walk to the stone bridge together and leave Miss Stapleford and my sister to continue their talk without us.'

'Of course,' answered the reverend, motioning to his wife to join him. Anton rose, then hesitated.

'I'm sure you have many important things to discuss, so if you will excuse me, I shall remain and await you here . . .' then, glancing at Sophie, 'with possibly more of your excellent tea?'

'Why, of course, my lord,' she said.

'But, Anton . . .' fumed Guy.

Anton waved his hand. 'Do not fuss, Guy. I shall be well looked after.'

Sophie's composure did not falter as she served the *comte* with more tea, but she was anxious that his presence might deprive her of an intimate talk with Lady Elizabeth. When he declined to join the walk to the bridge, she had noted the earl's annoyance and concluded this was not in accordance with his plans. She learned that the Comte Anton-Alexandre de Saint-Gabriel was a friend who had arrived at Adversane unexpectedly. He was handsome, with London airs and engaging dark eyes. She had never met anyone like him but, despite that, she was determined he would not interfere with *her* plans. How could she isolate the Lady Elizabeth to herself?

Suddenly, the door burst open. In a state of high excitement, Gus and Gussie came romping in.

'Oh dear,' said Sophie.

'How *chic* they are with their spots!' Anton exclaimed, rising to engage with them.

'They are not usually allowed in here,' said Sophie sternly. 'They should be in the garden.'

'Allow me to take them there, Miss Stapleford,' Anton volunteered.

'Oh, thank you. But they will exhaust you,' Sophie warned.

'Never!'

'Gus responds to stick-throwing, my lord,' added Sophie, by way of encouragement.

'Then he will not be disappointed. Come, Gus, with me,' he called, walking quickly from the room.

Gus and Gussie obeyed with alacrity and followed Anton into the garden. From the window, Sophie saw that the *comte* was immediately occupied in searching for sticks while Gus bounded about him. Sophie smiled to herself. Dogs to the rescue, she thought.

'I am glad of this opportunity to talk to you, Miss Stapleford. It would have been difficult to discuss private matters in the presence of the *comte* and I am thankful he has chosen to play with the dalmatians,' said Beth, gesturing for Sophie to sit with her on the settle.

'I have been waiting for this moment,' said Sophie softly, taking her place beside Beth.

Beth took her hand. 'That dress is so becoming on you, my dear, the colour so perfect. You have inherited the fine looks of your mother. I saw her on only two occasions, one being her wedding-day. On that day she radiated such joy that it gave an extra dimension to her loveliness. You have that quality, too. Are you happy, Miss Stapleford?'

'I—er . . . Yes, or perhaps no. I have had no news of my father and long for his return.'

'That is understandable. My brother is pursuing enquiries in the hope of relieving your mind. He fears you are lonely at the manor house without the benefit of contacts you would enjoy in a family.'

'That is so. I am either with the very old or very young. My days are spent pleasantly but of late . . .'

'Yes?'

'I have been curiously melancholy. Perhaps this can be put to loneliness.'

'My brother is right in his judgement, then?'

Sophie bowed her head as she felt her cheeks blushing at the thought of the earl voicing such concerns for her. Beth did not seek affirmation. She reached for Sophie's other hand and held them both.

'I think you should leave the manor house for a short time and come as my guest to Rothervale House. Sir Toby brings many visitors from London and foreign parts. You should meet such people and help me entertain them, if you are willing. As a family still in mourning our social engagements have been minimal but as time passes, some prudent gatherings would not be amiss. My brother wishes you to take your place in society as the daughter of Captain Sir John Stapleford, his very lovely daughter, so that your father will be proud of you when he returns. What do you think?'

Sophie raised her head. 'Do you mean that you would bestow me at Rothervale?'

'Yes,' Beth smiled. 'I would so welcome you.'

There was a silence. 'How very kind you are,' Sophie whispered.

Beth suddenly withdrew her hands and rose to stand by the chimney-piece.

'But there is something that may deter you,' she said.

'What is that?'

'Benjie and Harriet, my eight-year-old twins. They are full of tricks.'

Sophie laughed. 'Oh, a real family. The twins would not deter me at all. I have a certain hesitation in meeting people from London. I possess no knowledge of conduct or converse with such people.'

Beth smiled. 'I think it likely that such people would find the beautiful Miss Stapleford charming, and in no wise capable of offence or displeasure in the slightest degree.'

Sophie left her seat and joined Beth. Persuaded by her generous invitation, she knew she would accept if only to please the earl who had initiated these matters in her interest. Formality vanished as the ladies chatted and arranged for the safe bestowal of Nell, the dogs and Jet. The coach-house at Rothervale could accommodate the hackney and carriages. The transition would take place over the next week or two.

A thought occurred to Sophie. 'What of my tutors?'

'My brother has found them a situation with a private school in Somerset. They cannot refuse, the terms are favourable. He is informing them of it at this moment, and is arranging for reliable retainers to occupy the manor house in your absence.'

The earl had neglected nothing in the affair, thought Sophie with admiration. Contentment so invaded her that in place of relief at her tutors moving so far away, she was struck by wistfulness. She resolved to finish her watercolour of the manor house to present to the Reverend Lachbone, and would make a pomander for his wife. She knew Mrs Lachbone would be happy to go to Somerset, well beyond the reach of Hynde Hallam.

It was not long before sounds of pleasant converse heralded the return of Guy in company with the Reverend and Mrs Lachbone. They appeared well pleased, and Sophie guessed they had no objection to the termination of their service.

Guy looked askance at his sister, who

nodded imperceptibly. Sophie approached him and bobbed a diminutive curtsy.

'I have much to thank you for, my lord.'

'It is my duty as your guardian,' he said, 'thanks are not necessary.'

Sophie's pale-blue eyes met the serious grey and held them as she spoke softly.

'I think they are, my lord, and I shall thank you again and again, and again.'

Under her steady gaze he appeared disconcerted, and looked away. Suddenly, he asked: 'Where is the Comte de Saint-Gabriel?'

'He is playing with the dogs in the garden,' said Beth.

'We did not see him there, neither did we see the dogs,' said Guy.

They went outdoors searching, but soon returned as there was no sign of him.

'Perhaps he is somewhere in the house,' said Sophie.

She left the back drawing-room and began to look into the front rooms. The door to her father's room was slightly ajar and there she found the *comte*, slumped in an armchair.

'I am very unhappy, Miss Stapleford,' he said mournfully.

The late sun shone through the window, its fading rays brightening the captain's collection of sextants and nautical instruments. The *comte's* right hand hovered over the large terrestrial globe set beside him, his long pale fingers aiding its slow murmuring rotation.

For a moment Sophie watched in silence, wondering what could have caused her guest such dejection as was evident in his entire comportment. Then she spoke softly.

'I am sorry, my lord, that you feel so. Can we do anything to help?'

He leapt to his feet, leaving the globe spinning, and stood with arms akimbo before a full-length portrait of the captain.

'It grieves me to think that here I sit in *his* room while he is kept a prisoner in *my* country. Here are his books, denied to him. Here are his charts, denied to him. Here is his daughter—*très, très charmante*—denied to him!' He turned to face her. 'Can you feel the bitter irony of it?'

There was a sudden constriction in her throat. She knew her eyes were brimming, but not on her account—on his! How very sad, she thought, cursing the fates that had led him to this room.

'You must hate me that I am here!' he cried.

She shook her head, lowering it to rest upon her hands clasped across her breast.

'I can but speculate on the circumstances which forced you into exile here. Tragedy is there, I am sure.' She looked up. 'I could not hate you, my lord, and my welcome to you at this house is sincere and enduring.'

'*C'est un ange!*' he exclaimed, moving to confront her. Bowing low, he took her hand and pressed it to his lips. Glancing up at her, he whispered, 'I am yours to command, Miss Stapleford.' He stood upright and released her hand, brushing back a lock of dark hair which had fallen over his brow. As he did so, a ruby ring on his finger flashed red.

Sophie, now calm, said: 'My lord, you do me honour, and you have my gratitude.'

'I do not speak lightly for I could be of service. I am often called to Hartwell House in Buckinghamshire, where my sovereign King Louis the Eighteenth keeps his Court. Many in France support the Bourbon cause, and I shall make enquiries about your father and attempt to gain news of him when next I am at Hartwell. Meanwhile, accept this as a token of our understanding and my high regard of you, Miss Stapleford.'

He removed his ruby ring, took her hand and placed the ring in her palm, enclosing it with her fingers. His eyes sought hers.

'Oh, there is no need . . .' she remonstrated, trying to withdraw her hand.

'Please take it and keep it, I beg of you.'

She shook her head, frowning to demonstrate her discomfiture. Unwittingly, she had permitted the *comte* to engage in what she perceived as an unnecessary advance.

He stood close and placed his other hand over hers that held the ring fast. Her breath quickened. Near panic seized her as a tense silence ensued.

'Give the ring back, Miss Stapleford!'

The command came loud and clear from the doorway, allowing no choice. The tall figure of Lord Adversane stood at the threshold of the room. The air of nonchalance had vanished. Direct engagement was manifest in his posture and countenance.

Sophie's relief was immediate as the earl calmly approached, took the ring from her and returned it to the *comte* with a slight bow.

Anton coloured, shrugging as he replaced the ring upon his finger.

'As you wish, Guy.'

'It is time to join the others and prepare for our departure,' said the earl, taking Sophie's trembling hand and placing it upon his arm. Gently he rested his free hand upon hers in a gesture of reassurance, and led her from the room.

The farewells were brief, with the *comte* coldly polite and first to take his seat in the coach. The earl exchanged good wishes with the Reverend and Mrs Lachbone, while Lady Elizabeth embraced Sophie, hoping to meet soon at Rothervale.

The earl raised his hat and bent over Sophie's hand. Cool grey eyes regarded her.

'If it be in my power to prevent, none shall take advantage of you while I am your guardian,' he said. He held her gaze as he replaced his hat and turned to help his sister to her seat. With a final bow, he sprang nimbly on to the foot-board as the coach surged forward.

Sophie sighed pleasurably. Her circumstances had changed over the teacups. She no longer felt alone.

Guy placed his hat on an overhead rack in the coach and settled into a corner seat. Beth leaned back against the squabs, looking at Guy in silence for a moment.

'You told me many things about Miss Stapleford but you did not mention the most striking impression you must have gained,' she observed.

'What may that be?'

'You did not tell me what a beauty she is. She has natural grace, fine features, remarkable eyes together with excellent dress-sense and deportment.'

'Not apparent at my first encounter with her,' he retorted. 'Are you implying that given the perfections you have observed, a sojourn in your care is unnecessary?'

Beth smiled. 'Pho! Why so sensitive? It simply means that my task is half-completed. She is ready for company. Many young nobles will apprehend you to offer for her.'

'Then it's as well we are a family in mourning and the opportunities will be few,' he snapped. 'Any offers that are made must be refused.'

'They should be considered at least, Guy,' said Anton, stretching out his booted legs. 'It is only fair.'

'I beg to differ,' said Guy. 'Remember, my

responsibility for Miss Stapleford ends with the return of her father. As her guardian, I have not the slightest intention of considering any suitor however appropriate to her station. That is a matter for the captain.'

'But many will be charmed by her beauty, and then there is the Rossington fortune when she comes of age. A full measure of attractions, I am bound to say,' said Beth.

'What is this Rossington fortune? Sir Henry imparted nothing of this to me,' said Guy.

'It is well known that she will inherit the proceeds of the Rossington estate through her mother's line,' said Beth.

Anton laughed. 'Do not say you were unaware of it, Guy! Surely that was your reason for agreeing to the guardianship.'

'You would never comprehend my reason, Anton, so further speculation is fruitless. The fact of this Rossington inheritance adds strength to my resolve in refusing to entertain any suitors for her hand.'

'That does not mean she must be kept under lock and key,' added Beth. 'She has had a trifling life at the manor house, and I would be pleased to have her beside me for the few occasions we shall entertain.'

'She is certainly a beauty, and the fortune will attract,' mused Anton.

Guy did not respond. He sat hunched in the corner of the coach, elbow resting upon crossed knee and hand cupping his chin. How could he have been blind to the charms of Miss Stapleford when first he saw her? He had the distinct feeling that the fault was not entirely on his part.

Gazing out of the window, he thought about the guardianship. He had assumed it would simply be a matter of satisfying material needs, and had arranged for Beth to attend to all the refinements, sparing him direct involvement with his ward; but the incident with Anton and the ring had given him pause. He must stand by her at such times offering protection and guidance.

He was also aware that her proximity at Rothervale would mean a deeper association with his own family and lead to more encounters with the young lady. In this way he could evaluate her progress and keep her father apprised. Indeed, it would be fitting for him to escort her to the occasional function. That which had at first appeared to be a millstone upon him, could become a pleasant diversion and he envisaged such duties as distinctly agreeable.

He sighed contentedly and relaxed his position. Glancing at Beth, he was surprised to disturb her close regard of him—a regard tinged with sisterly amusement. He decided to say nothing further on the subject of Miss Stapleford.

The Manor House

Every room in the manor house was darkened by the shadows of early morning and familiar items of furniture were transformed by holland covers. Sophie, already in bonnet and cloak, had one more task to do before Seb arrived to take her to Rothervale.

All was quiet as she sped up the stairs and entered the lumber-room. She threw back the lid of the chest and felt under the stored dresses until the board covers of Mrs Lachbone's portfolio came to her hand. She opened it and saw several paintings and pencil sketches featuring landscape in amazing detail. The hamlet of Nether Cherry and surrounding forests were pictured and, of great importance, thought Sophie, dated and signed. It was no wonder that Hynde Hallam sought to destroy this evidence proving his unauthorized activities.

She replaced the items neatly, and securely tied the portfolio tapes. After closing the chest, she rose and carried the portfolio under her left arm, covering it entirely with her cloak, then entered the hall where a valise stood with her other band-boxes. She stooped to open the valise and paused on hearing a carriage come to a stop outside. Thinking it to be Seb, she continued to wrestle with the hasp, when the door opened. She looked up. Towering above her was the black-clad figure of Hynde

Hallam. Sophie drew breath as she rose, and clutched more tightly the portfolio, mercifully hidden under her cloak.

'Good morning, Miss Stapleford,' said Hallam stiffly. He regarded the gathered luggage. 'I see you are soon to depart. I have come to call upon the Reverend Lachbone to wish him well.'

'Oh,' said Sophie. 'The Reverend and his wife left some four days ago, Mr Hallam.'

A deep frown creased his brow, but only momentarily.

'I was misinformed,' he said softly.

He turned abruptly and strode to the staircase. With one foot on the bottom stair and a hand on the banister, he stood silently looking up to the landings as if listening for sounds of occupancy.

Sophie stared in surprise. 'There is no one upstairs, Mr Hallam.'

'I know that,' he said, maintaining his stance. 'I am thinking that the manor house would provide an excellent abode for myself.'

'His lordship has arranged for Mr and Mrs Parker to occupy the house in my absence. They move in tomorrow,' said Sophie.

'Parker! Did you say *Parker?*' he demanded, striding towards her. 'Is that the same gentleman who was butler to the old earl?'

'I think it likely. Lord Adversane is re-employing loyal retainers such as the Parkers,' said Sophie pointedly.

'Hrrmph,' he snorted, stepping aside to the captain's room. He threw the door wide open. 'This would make a suitable office for me with one or two staff.'

Sophie hastily joined him at the door, endeavouring to close it. He resolutely kept it open with his foot, a sardonic smile fleeting over his face.

'This room is my father's, Mr Hallam,' said Sophie, conscious of a tremor in her voice.

He laughed. 'You cannot nurture the futile thought that your father will ever use it again!'

'I do, and he will,' she retorted. 'My absence is temporary, a matter of months, and his lordship would never terminate my father's lease in the circumstances.'

'His lordship may have no choice,' Hallam replied airily.

'What do you mean?'

He turned and walked slowly back to the hall.

'Lord Adversane is living on borrowed money. He is here dodging his creditors. Soon he will return to London and when he does, Adversane will be lost to him.'

'I don't believe you. Lord Adversane is committed to his inheritance and all attendant duties.'

'Think what you will. He is here hiding from debt-collectors and jilted females,' said Hallam.

'Jilted females?' sputtered Sophie,

immediately regretting her overreaction.

Hallam smiled. 'So it's said.'

Sophie recovered her composure.

'Listening to rumours and trusting in their truth gives cold comfort, Mr Hallam.'

Suddenly there were shouts outside and the sound of a carriage on the gravelled approach. Sophie rushed out to see Seb with the Adversane coach, and Jem rising from the box-seat. Mr Hallam chose to leave. He hastened to his black curricle and, with whip cracking, was soon out of sight.

With relief, Sophie returned to open the valise and placed the portfolio safely within. Seb greeted her and offered his arm to lead her to the coach. She was delighted to see the staff had gathered in line to bid her farewell.

'God's blessings on you, Miss Sophie!' they called, and an abundance of posies dropped in her lap as she joined Nell in the coach.

There was an impairment to this happy departure. As the coach picked up speed, she glanced back at the manor house, still in shadow. She tried not to think of Hallam occupying her cherished home, and determined to air her views with his lordship at the first opportunity.

CHAPTER FIVE

Rothervale House, May 1812

Sophie walked hand-in-hand with the twins over dew-laden lawns, returning from a morning walk by the river. April had melted into May, and the countryside wore an ascendancy of blue as bluebells were joined by speedwell and bugle.

'Our birthday is very soon,' said Harriet. 'We always have a picnic by the river on our birthday.'

'Can you fish?' asked Benjie, gruffly.

'Oh, yes,' replied Sophie.

Benjie stopped short. 'I did not think you could fish.'

'Before my father went back to sea, we visited the river often. He taught me to cast for trout.'

'Then you must teach Benjie,' said Harriet. 'He is not very good.'

Benjie grimaced at Harriet. 'You never fish at all!'

'I shall help you, Benjie. That's a promise,' said Sophie, taking steps to continue their walk.

As they approached the house, their governess hailed them from the terrace.

'Morning lessons,' groaned Harriet.

'Let's race to the house!' cried Benjie, making sure he had a head start.

The morning dew had soaked Sophie's shoes and hose, so she returned to her room to change. For a moment, she lingered by the window, charmed by the sparkling waters of the river and the blue flash of a kingfisher.

Six weeks had passed since her arrival at Rothervale. She was happy in this beautiful house. Within the first week Beth had taken her to the silk-mill at Whitchurch, where lengths were selected to expand her wardrobe. She readily responded to Beth's instructions as to refinement, and slipped with ease into the new routine, enjoying the change both in her person and in her perception. Not only did she want her father to be proud of her on his return, but wished also to be worthy of the beneficence bestowed upon her by Lord Adversane.

Soon after her arrival, Beth had given her a letter from him. It expressed the hope that she be settled happily at Rothervale House, and that he would call to see her as time allowed. She cherished the letter, reading it daily and looked eagerly for his appearance. Eventually she mastered her expectations by reason of his preoccupation with the estate.

Her riding excursions were now in company with Beth and Toby. Correctly habited, veils covered her face, recommended by Beth to shield her from unfashionable high colour. At first she had been shy in the presence of Sir Tobias Dallimore MP, but now she welcomed the sound of his booming voice. He engaged her interest in the issues of the day, and delighted her in his praise of her parents whom he had known and respected.

She turned from the window, drew on fresh hose and slippers, then tidied her hair before going downstairs to see Beth. As she entered the withdrawing-room, Beth beckoned to join her at the table, where she was already pouring coffee.

'Housekeepers,' said Beth, 'present me with lists, lists and more lists. This house could not run without lists.'

'You are a mistress-of-household I admire,' said Sophie.

'I'm fortunate in my staff and that makes all the difference,' said Beth, handing a cup of coffee to Sophie, 'but domestic matters should not concern you. You are young, and should have other things on your mind. Soirees, balls, the opera and beaux!'

'Such things do not enter my mind,' said Sophie softly, 'at least not to any extent.'

'Then we shall have to make amends,' said Beth, smiling. 'I have engaged an Italian music-tutor for the twins as it's time they had some musical instruction. It would be a good idea for you to take advantage of his presence and develop your own talents in that art.'

Sophie clasped her hands. 'That is

wonderful! I have missed musical interludes with my father, and would be happy to join with the tutor to aid his teaching of the twins.'

'He will arrive after the twins' birthday and shall stay for some weeks until he moves on to another engagement in the county. He is the tenor, Signor Basilio Bordoni.'

'How very Italian, and a singer, too!' said Sophie.

There was a silence as both sipped their coffee. Then Beth spoke.

'Our period of mourning is advancing and it may be fitting to plan a musical evening. Toby might bring a guest or two, and we could invite our neighbours. Perhaps by then you could take part in it.'

Sophie coloured. 'I have never performed in company. My talent is limited, I fear.'

'We shall allow the *signor* to be the judge of that,' said Beth.

Sophie shrugged, musing that her father had always praised her singing but she discounted this as paternal partiality.

'I almost forgot,' said Beth suddenly. 'Toby is to stay with Guy at Adversane for a day or two. Somewhere I have noted the items he wishes to take with him.' She opened a large book and ruffled through a sheaf of papers.

'Another list?' asked Sophie amusedly.

Beth smiled. 'A necessary one, Sophie. He wishes me to pack surveying-instruments as well as his smallclothes. He is to assist Guy in

81

assessing spoliation of his lands preparatory to a claim.'

'Oh,' said Sophie, thinking of Mrs Lachbone's portfolio safely tucked away in her valise upstairs.

'Toby will be returning in good time for the twins' ninth birthday picnic. I hope Guy is able to come. He usually does. I have a list for that, too!' said Beth, triumphantly waving a sheet of paper.

Sophie was silent. There might be an opportunity to give Lord Adversane the portfolio at the fishing picnic, as obviously he would be looking for proof prior to a claim.

Beth continued to search through her papers. Then she looked up.

'I have a surprise for you,' she said. 'I accepted an invitation to call upon our neighbours, Sir Hugh and Lady Wardyne, tomorrow evening. Their son has joined the army and is soon to be sent to foreign parts. It will be a small gathering and I think you should come along with us, Sophie.'

'Oh, no. I must remain,' said Sophie, startled.

'Why should you remain? The Wardynes are a charming family and it is an excellent opportunity for your first venture to a social function. Please come. I know Toby will insist upon it.'

Sophie bit her lip, then nodded.

Beth smiled. 'I know you are wondering

what to wear, Sophie. The French cambric with its new trimming will be appropriate. It is not a grand affair.'

Sophie smiled. 'You read my thoughts, Beth.'

'I'm also planning a visit to cousin Arabella in Brighton and afterwards for sojourns in Cheltenham and Bath. Social delights await you and I know there will be escorts a-plenty!'

'How can you be so certain?'

'You are unaware of the potency of your own beauty, Sophie. My brother was quite put out, and do you not recall the reaction of Anton, Comte de Saint-Gabriel, on first sight of you?'

'I recall that I did not welcome his approach.'

Beth smiled. 'You will learn to ward off such unwelcome advances with ease and dignity, Sophie.'

Sophie was occupied in recurrent thought of that incident in the captain's room. In retrospect it seemed to her now that a finger of light had fortuitously touched her noble rescuer with a sudden evanescent magic.

That night she slept fitfully, dreading on the morrow the evening visit to Dynes Park. She was unused to social calls and, despite Beth's reassurances, could not deny that she would prefer to remain at Rothervale. As the day progressed, she allowed Nell to dress her hair. Later, she marked with pleasure how the lilac-velvet spencer, a gift from Beth, perfectly complemented her gown.

As dusk fell, she joined Beth and Toby, bonneted and cloaked, in the coach for the short journey to Dynes Park. Now quiet and composed, she listened to titbits of gossip about the Wardynes; but suddenly, Toby said:

'I wonder if Guy will be there. He's a boyhood friend of Barty Wardyne.'

'It's likely, I suppose,' Beth replied.

Sophie closed her eyes. This was entirely unexpected. She felt herself trembling, her composure ebbing away. The prospect of meeting her guardian at a social function implying parity, was daunting. She was anxious not to disappoint him. No, she argued with herself, *my life has changed, and I shall face him with confidence.*

The gates opened and the winding drive ended in a large circle, illuminated with twinkling lights. She smiled as her eyes met Beth's.

'I think we shall share a very pleasant evening, Beth,' she said; but refrained from voicing a concluding thought: *whether my guardian is there, or not.*

The salon, rosy and intimate, reflected the warmth in the greeting of their hosts, Sir Hugh and Lady Wardyne. Gentle arpeggios of sound came from a harp, played by a silver-haired lady in a far corner. Without staring too closely at those chatting together, it was evident to

Sophie that her guardian was not present. She admitted to disappointment and knew she would suffer a tremulous wait for his arrival.

The popularity of Beth and Toby was obvious and soon Barty, the handsome son, splendid in his regimentals, insisted on being introduced to Sophie. He proved a heaven-sent diversion for her. She enjoyed his converse since, as a cavalry subaltern, his interest in horses was paramount. His experiences, humorously related, promoted laughter and he attached himself as her escort to the refreshment tables and throughout the evening.

Sophie and Barty seated themselves with his parents. They were joined by Beth and Toby as liqueurs and sweetmeats were served. There followed much teasing of his son by Sir Hugh on the directive that the 10th Hussars should wear moustaches.

'Would you think such a flocculus necessary to improve military prowess, Sir Toby?' asked Sir Hugh, smiling broadly.

Sir Toby shook his head as Barty flushed, but took it all in good part.

'One must conform to the uniform, Papa!' he replied. 'You wouldn't have me do otherwise.'

A footman bent to Lady Wardyne's ear, whereupon she rose to greet a young lady who had just entered the salon. She returned accompanied by her. The gentlemen rose as

Lady Wardyne made the introduction.

'Please welcome a relative of mine from London, Lady Charlotte Cotterell.'

After the introductions, with a rustling of bronze silk and gauze, Lady Charlotte sat in a proffered chair next to Barty. Sophie judged her over-dressed, over-jewelled and over-rouged for the occasion, but nodded sympathetically as Lady Wardyne explained the circumstances of her visit. Her London home, apparently, had become a building site since her benefactor insisted on modifying and increasing the number of apartments.

'You must find the countryside a benefice to you in the meantime, Lady Charlotte. The very fields and woodlands are calming and inspiring in the changes wrought by the seasons. Do you not agree?' said Sophie.

Lady Charlotte turned to regard her with half-closed amber eyes.

'All my friends know that I dislike life in the country, Miss Stapleford. I am sentenced to remain here for some months and already miss my daily social calls. I can hardly wait to return and am counting the days 'til my release.'

There was a silence. Beth appeared to be closely examining the contents of her liqueur glass. Sophie, embarrassed on Lady Charlotte's behalf for her ungraciousness towards her hostess, glanced at Lady Wardyne who appeared unperturbed. Sir Hugh smothered a cough, and summoned a footman to replenish the glasses. Lady Charlotte addressed Sophie.

'My observations tell me that you have no idea of London life, Miss Stapleford.'

Sophie smiled. 'You are correct, Lady Charlotte, and I hope that that will soon be remedied; but I don't think I should ever *prefer* it to country life.'

'That would depend upon how well you are received, your connections and so forth,' said Lady Charlotte, ending the conversation by furiously working her fan.

Barty turned to Sophie. 'Perhaps we could go for a riding jaunt together, Miss Stapleford, provided I am not summoned to the Peninsula in the meantime.'

Sophie smiled agreement, grateful for the change of subject. Barty was suggesting routes they could follow, when he was called away.

'A late arrival, I think,' he whispered.

She watched him leaving the salon with a sprightly stride. He would be an amusing companion, she thought, but was wistful in knowing that he could be called to war. She looked sadly at Lady Wardyne, happily chatting to Beth, and pitied the dreaded uncertainty that would haunt the family while Barty was thus engaged. Such feelings were well known to her.

Suddenly, her eyes were drawn to the opening salon-doors where Barty stood with Lord Adversane. He smiled, acknowledging her with a bow of his head. Her heart throbbed at the sight of his sombre though elegant presence; but nothing prepared her for the reaction of Lady Charlotte. She appeared to tumble from her chair in a flurry of silks and, with arms outstretched, scrambled towards Lord Adversane in a most ungainly fashion. All heads turned.

'O my beloved!' she exclaimed, seizing his arm. 'What an extraordinary coincidence!'

'Not exactly a coincidence,' murmured Lady Wardyne. 'Dear Charlotte had sought out most of the grand estates adjacent to Adversane, which included Dynes Park. She invited herself, claiming a tenuous relationship with me to justify it. Her sole purpose was to meet Lord Adversane.'

'Hers is one name I was not aware of,' answered Beth in an undertone.

Sophie watched as her guardian promptly removed Lady Charlotte's proprietorial grip on his arm and distanced himself before formally bending over her hand. Beth and Lady Wardyne left their seats and approached him to relieve his obvious discomposure. He greeted them warmly, leading them back to their chairs while Barty escorted a flushed Lady Charlotte to the refreshment tables in the anteroom.

Sophie was about to rise but Lord Adversane playfully prevented her from doing so, taking her hand and raising it to his lips.

'Your presence here is a most pleasant surprise, Miss Stapleford,' he whispered, his grey eyes silvery with amusement. 'Surprises are more welcome than shocks in certain circumstances, are they not?'

She smiled in response to his oblique reference to the earlier incident. In truth, she was saddened by it. Lady Charlotte's behaviour indicated supreme confidence in his regard of her, but a gross misunderstanding had occurred. She recalled Hallam's reference to her guardian's 'jilted females'. Was it possible that Lady Charlotte was included in that company?

The deep sounds of the harp echoed her dejection. The music hung on the air for a moment, then gradually faded as the lady harpist rested her hands on the strings, her head bowed. A footman appeared at her side, offering her a drink. Slowly she looked up, took the glass and sipped from it. Sophie crossed the salon and approached her.

'I had to come and thank you for the so-lovely melodies you have played to entertain us this evening. There is something about harp music that makes the mind dance, a necessary accompaniment to conversation at such a gathering,' said Sophie softly.

The lady's eyes shone. 'How very kind you are. I simply enjoy playing. Lady Wardyne is my niece and she harbours me at Dynes Park. It is my pleasure to help at her soirées.'

'And your name is?'

'Miss Emily Beckwith. And yours?'

'Miss Sophia Stapleford. I am also kindly harboured at Rothervale.'

Miss Beckwith was about to reply, when she rose abruptly and bobbed a curtsy. Sophie suddenly realized Lord Adversane had joined them.

'Oh, my lord,' she said, 'I had to thank Miss Beckwith for her playing. I thought it was delightful.'

'As a late arrival, the little I have heard puts me in harmony with you both.' He smiled.

He nodded to Miss Beckwith, then took Sophie's hand.

'The coaches are lining up and all are gathering in the hall. Allow me to escort you there, Miss Stapleford.'

He placed her hand on his arm and, with a parting nod to Miss Beckwith, they walked through the salon to the hall. There was a hubbub with guests preparing to depart, and the opening and closing of the porch doors allowed draughts to play with the candleflames in the sconces.

Barty joined them and persuaded Guy to delay his departure so that they could play billiards. He performed a brisk military salute to Sophie.

'I will ascertain when I am to leave, Miss Stapleford,' he said, 'but before that we'll share a ride where there are some fine gallops.'

Guy stiffened, frowning.

'Now, Barty, you must see she comes to no harm,' he said.

'Of course,' Barty replied.

'Perhaps you may wish to join us.'

Guy shrugged. 'Perhaps I may.'

Sophie meanwhile had put on her bonnet and cloak.

'There's Sir Toby standing by the coach,' said Lord Adversane. 'I will take you down to him and at the same time discuss his visit to Adversane.' He lowered his voice. 'Your approach to Miss Beckwith was a gesture of spontaneous kindness, Miss Stapleford. I am impressed.'

She smiled with delight at his comment as Sir Toby took her hand to aid her entry to the coach. After a chat with Sir Toby, Guy left to find Beth. She was standing by the porch ready to leave. She beckoned to Guy who leapt up the steps and clasped her hands.

'Beth,' he said, 'there has not been a word exchanged between us since your welcome intervention. I am staying to play billiards with Barty, and . . .' he added softly, 'to console a certain young lady.'

'Lady Charlotte, I presume. Is she a new interest, Guy?'

'No, never of any interest whatsoever.'

'I would not have thought so.'

'She is anxious to marry any earl, marquess

91

or duke. That is the limit of her interest in me. She has a want of nicety which greatly displeases me; unlike, for example, Miss Stapleford.' He kissed her on the cheek. 'I shall expect Toby at Adversane within a week.' He left her and returned to the house.

Beth began her walk to the coach. She pondered Guy's remarks about Lady Charlotte and wished Sophie had been present to hear them. Beth had noted her crestfallen mien after Lady Charlotte's effusive greeting of Guy. In recalling Sophie's ardent defence of life in the country, Beth thought some encouragement in a certain quarter might persuade Guy to remain at Adversane.

In the billiard-room at Dynes Park, Guy adjusted the marker board prior to another game. His enthusiasm for billiards had waned. Why did he feel disquiet at the thought of Miss Stapleford's riding assignment with the comely and dashing Barty? It was a cue to take more interest in his ward.

Adversane House

Guy stood on the porch steps watching the main gates opening to admit Sir Toby Dallimore riding his panniered cob. He trotted down the drive to the house, while Guy summoned a footman and a groom to ease the arrival of the corpulent rider and his portly mount.

Later, after the baggage had been unloaded and the cob cosseted and stabled, Guy led Toby to the octagon room where refeshments were served. An extra table had been installed so that Toby could inspect the maps of the demesne lands.

Toby withdrew his spectacles, placed them firmly on his nose and leaned over the maps.

'Hm,' he said. 'I didn't realize how vast an estate this is.'

'I have it in mind we should spend a night at the Falcon inn. I'm told it's a salubrious hostelry conveniently placed at the extreme western bounds. In that way, we could rise at daybreak and spend an entire day in the area. What do you think, Toby?'

Toby nodded vigorously. 'Kinder to the horses, too.' He took off his spectacles and faced Guy. 'So you think your father's steward is at the bottom of this unauthorized exploitation?'

'I'm certain of it.'

'Why was a steward, whose duties are normally restricted to the house, permitted to act as land agent?'

'I've asked myself that question many times, and can only presume that when father took to his bed, the steward extended his range of duties for his own benefit.'

'Surely there was another upper servant who could have brought this to your father's notice?'

'That person would have been Mr Parker, his butler; but he was swiftly dismissed by Hallam, as were other loyal servants,' said Guy. He paused, then sighing audibly added: 'I curse my own blinkered persuasion that all was well. The least I can do now is assess the damage and lodge a claim.'

Toby clapped a hand on Guy's shoulder.

'Then let no grass grow under our heels, Guy. Could we reach the Falcon by this evening and stay a second night? My appetite's whetted for some tavern ale, as well as bringing Hallam to book.'

'Then let's to the challenge,' said Guy, laughing as he went to the door.

Guy arranged with Lewis, his valet, for the immediate departure of a mounted footman to travel ahead to the Falcon so that suitable rooms could be made ready for them.

They dallied on their journey, often dismounting to explore on foot the ugly tracks left by wagons removing the felled giants of the forest. At one point, Guy halted and shook his head, perplexed.

'There should be a hamlet hereabouts marked on the map as Nether Cherry; but there's no sign of habitation.' Pressing on, they came across recently wrecked cottage ruins amid the ground cover of renewed forest growth.

'Zooks, Guy!' exclaimed Toby.

Guy lost count of the times Toby spat out this minced oath to vent his anger. Yet neither oath nor words could express Guy's outrage at the desolation around him.

'They shall pay,' he muttered, 'and the moneys gained will restore the hamlet and all else besides. I shall make this estate an Arcadian delight with places for public enjoyment, the gravel pits transformed into ornamental lakes stocked with fish, a grotto by the cascade . . .' He set his mind against the weakness of guilt, convinced that in the active pursuit of his dream lay expiation.

They found their horses and returned to the road in silence. By now it was twilight, and a breeze stirred the ox-eye daisies which shone like shillings in the darkening meadows. Soon Guy saw through the trees the candlelit windows of the Falcon and, as they entered the yard, ostlers approached to attend the horses.

A lantern-bearing landlord, Mr Silas Oakover, stood with his wife by the chequered pillars of the porch, smiling a welcome. Mrs Oakover bobbed a curtsy to both while their host ushered them into a private snug at the rear of the inn.

Toby's thirst for tavern ale was satisfied as he immediately insisted on their both downing a tankard. Then they were served with a supper of cold veal and tongue, tarts and cream, toasted cheese and butter. To follow, Guy ordered port-wine and brandy which was

95

brought in by the landlord himself.

'Give me leave, sir,' said Guy, 'to express our thanks for the pleasure we have received and the proprieties observed at your establishment.'

'And tell your lady wife that the meal was delectable', added Toby.

Mr Oakover beamed as he inclined his head in acknowledgment.

'We are pleased and honoured that you so grace our house. With your leave, my lord, may I put a question?'

'What may it be?' asked Guy.

'When shall Mr Hallam be this way again, my lord?'

'Was he often this way?'

'Indeed yes, my lord. For some years he's scooped out gravel and shorn forests with helpers from places far afield. He lodged here betimes and although he demanded service as a man of consequence, I fear that he was not so. I can present sheaves of unpaid bills to his account, my lord.'

Guy caught Toby's eye as he said:

'Tot them all. I will see that they are paid. Entertain him no more, my good sir.'

'That I will not. There are many hereabouts impoverished by these workings and made homeless by the destruction of Nether Cherry. They are forced on to the parish, my lord.'

Guy recounted his plans for the restoration of the estate and the entire hamlet, saying there would be tasks a-plenty, and no one seeking work would be turned away.

'That is my serious undertaking,' he concluded.

Oakover's eyes glistened in the candlelight.

'Bless you, my lord. I will spread the good tidings,' he said, bowing as he withdrew.

'That will disturb Hallam, should the good tidings reach him,' observed Toby, pursing his lips.

The next day, word had spread that the young earl was in the vicinity and had promised restitution. A good-natured crowd gathered outside the inn as Guy and Toby mounted their horses. Several hardy men followed them, on horseback and on foot, offering their detailed knowledge as to the land, its crops and trees, before spoliation.

Later, Guy hosted an impromptu celebration with those helpers in the taproom of the inn and reiterated his promise to them. That night he slept soundly and rose refreshed, eager to return and set his claim in motion.

The next morning they started their return to Adversane. An early mist concealed those damaged acres which they had explored, and forced a slow pace upon them.

'Let us talk about figures,' said Guy.

'Fifteen thousand guineas,' said Toby without hesitation. 'It's a good round sum for the extracted lumber and gravel, added to such items as Hallam's account with Oakover.'

'Fifteen thousand it shall be,' said Guy 'It will be ample for the restoration.'

'So you will inform Sir Henry Nancarrow of your conclusions and await his advice.'

'Precisely.'

'And what will you do about Hallam?'

'I shall dismiss him. Hallam has not been in the house since I took up residence. He remains in his quarters waiting for me to return to London.'

'There may be difficulties ahead.'

'None that are insurmountable,' answered Guy confidently. 'I am well served at the moment. I may re-employ Mr Parker, father's butler as soon as Miss Stapleford returns to the manor house where he is the present custodian.'

'Ah, Miss Stapleford, our Sophie,' said Toby, with a smile in his voice. 'She's a beauty and a delight in all the virtues of her sex, yet full of surprises.'

'I have not yet managed to visit her at Rothervale. I presume all is well.'

'Beth and the children worship her—and I'd go better than that. When we hold more social occasions she'll be pestered by swains, I'll warrant,' Toby replied with a chuckle.

Guy did not feel disposed to speculate on such matters concerning his ward, and changed the subject.

'I'd like to halt at Chadlett Hill to show you

my favourite view of the house and park.'

'It's the prettiest sight ever,' remarked Toby dreamily.

'So you know that view?'

'No, Guy. I meant that Sophie is the prettiest sight when instructing the twins in carriage-driving. She seats them either side of her in my phaeton and allows Benjie to take the ribbons in turn with Harriet.' Toby sighed. 'It's enchanting.'

On the home stretch, clouds curtained the day and winds teased the meadow grasses. Guy halted at the top of Chadlett Hill. Toby dismounted, and joined him in looking at the estate spread below them.

'Reverting to your praise of Miss Stapleford's driving activities, I know what I shall give the twins on their birthday,' said Guy.

'Not too costly, I hope.'

'Simply appropriate.'

After a short silence, Toby suddenly said: 'Guy, what do you see about five miles north of here? Stap me, it's cloudy but I can pick it out.'

Guy narrowed his eyes. After a moment, he said: ''Pon my honour, Toby, I can see nothing apart from Adversane church tower.'

Toby laughed. 'That's just what I wanted you to say, Adversane church tower, five miles from the place where we now stand.' Toby extended his arm and pointing towards the tower, added: 'In a straight line, we could have great sport. Have you heard of this new fad called steeplechase riding?'

'Yes, I have. It's challenging others to ride over the country, taking on gates, hedges, banks or whatever obstacle is met. Didn't it start in Ireland?'

'It did, and it was an Irish groom from Tattersall's told me of it. Mounts are usually hunters with a jumping ability, and it attracts the most daring of riders.'

Guy, impressed, reached for his field glass to survey the terrain. The fenced copses, banked lanes, ditches, and the ups and downs of the country would be an irresistible challenge.

'It would be a thrill if matched against a like rider and horse for a wager,' added Toby.

'That would be excellent sport,' said Guy, still holding the field glass to his eye. 'It's all Adversane land, except the field by the churchyard which belongs to Squire Budge.'

'I'll wager the squire will be the first contender,' said Toby.

Guy rammed his field glass into its case.

'I'll ask Seb to help in this. We'll place more hazards and try Brisket on it. Beginning of October is the time for it, Toby, just before cubbing. The Adversane steeplechase will be on the calendar!'

Toby remounted, and Guy turned Japhet to canter the last three miles to the house. He was exhilarated by the tasks he had set himself—to restore Nether Cherry and his lands, and create a steeplechase course; but, more pleasurable, to seek a small carriage and pony for the twins. He applauded Miss Stapleford's initiative in teaching them to handle a carriage and hoped, in developing that connection, she might be persuaded of his esteem.

CHAPTER SIX

Sophie sat by the window in her room, her workbox open and hands busily stitching. The twins were in the school-room with the governess, and Sophie took this opportunity to prepare their birthday gifts without intrusion. Hidden in the closet was the wicker creel for Benjie which an estate craftsman had made to Sophie's order. Now she was attaching the last flounce on to a dress for Primrose, Harriet's favourite wooden doll.

She severed the thread, and held up the little garment with its matching cap. Smiling, she knew Harriet would enjoy replacing Primrose's faded gingham with this dress of glistening silk in a hue to match her name. Sophie carefully folded both items and placed them in her workbox.

Suddenly she was aware of shouts in the

lower hall. She hastened to the landing where she saw a footman unlocking the outer door. In came Sir Toby, bellowing for assistance, with his hat askew and a screeching twin held captive under each arm. He dumped the twins unceremoniously as Sophie rushed down the stairs to welcome him home. Beth joined them and was swept into a warm embrace. Toby was relieved of his hat and topcoat by the footman and, linking arms with Beth and Sophie, guided them to the salon anteroom.

'Let's have a sup of wine together,' he suggested. 'I shall need it, for I have much to relate.'

'Then perhaps I should leave . . .' began Sophie. 'It must concern the family.'

Toby tightened his hold on her arm.

'Your father is a tenant at Adversane, is he not?'

'Yes—but . . .'

' 'Pon my soul, that qualifies. You're almost a member of the family, Sophie, so I'll not permit you to absent yourself,' said Toby with exaggerated authority.

'Best to remain, Sophie,' said Beth smiling, while summoning a footman to serve wine and cakes.

Sophie sipped her wine, listening intently to Sir Toby recounting his and Guy's exploits in assessing the plunder of Adversane lands.

'Guy thinks Hallam is the culprit, probably with associates,' he said. 'A claim will be lodged against him and the funds garnered shall not only reinstate the forests but also improve them, employing those who have suffered displacement.'

'I feel sorry for Guy,' said Beth. 'To inherit all this!'

Sophie put down her wine glass. She felt her cheeks burning as she said softly:

'I think I could help him establish his claim.'

There was a silence as they stared at her. She then told of her interview with Mrs Lachbone, Hallam's burning of her painting and his pressure on her to give up her other paintings.

'The hamlet of Nether Cherry is particularly featured in them,' she concluded.

'Phew!' sputtered Toby. 'The Lachbones have left Adversane, so where are these paintings?'

'Mrs Lachbone gave them to me so that I could pass them to Lord Adversane when the need arose.' She got to her feet. 'They are locked in my valise. I shall bring them to you, Sir Toby, and perhaps you will ensure that Lord Adversane sees them.'

She fled upstairs and returned breathless, bearing the portfolio. They gathered round a table to view the contents piece by piece. Sir Toby put on his spectacles to study them, exclaiming aloud when he recognized the once forested glades, now a wasteland. They were saddened to hear of the present state of

Nether Cherry. Mrs Lachbone's deft touch had caught the cottages in evening light with children running home, and chimney smoke rising to mingle with the tree-tops that sheltered the hamlet. They speculated at the work needed to restore it.

'A lifetime's commitment, I'll warrant,' said Toby, 'but I'll do all I can to help him.'

'As will I,' said Sophie thoughtfully. 'Those families of Nether Cherry will need assistance.'

'That will be in the future, Sophie,' added Beth. 'You have contributed already. Securing the paintings for Guy's use shows forethought. I'm sure he would agree with me.'

'No wonder Hallam was after 'em,' said Toby. 'I see each is inscribed with the date and time o' day. Guy will be forever grateful.'

'I have much to thank him for,' said Sophie quietly.

Toby returned to his armchair. He removed his spectacles and took a kerchief to polish them. After a moment he spoke.

'There's another development Guy is planning which would interest you, Sophie, with your knowledge of Adversane.'

'And what may that be?' she asked.

'Guy is intent on establishing a steeplechase run from Chadlett Hill to Adversane church tower.'

Sophie frowned. 'A steeplechase run?'

'It's a fad everyone's taking up—couple of chaps started it in Ireland some sixty years ago.

It's usually over four or five miles, without the necessity of fox and hounds. Wonderful sport for a wager between two or more riders. It's over Adversane land, and Guy's keen on it.'

Sophie brightened. 'How exciting! I'd love to ride the course on Jet.'

'Guy is keen to try Brisket on it,' said Toby, putting aside his spectacles and kerchief.

'That beautiful grey,' said Beth. 'He's a born jumper.'

'You'll soon know all about it. Guy will be here for the twins' birthday, at which time,' added Toby, 'I shall hand him this portfolio.'

*   *   *

It was Jem's appearance at Rothervale that made Sophie aware of Guy's gift to the twins. A carriage and pony had been driven from Adversane by Jem. The carriage was hidden in the barn at Rothervale, and one of the grooms led the pony to the home farm stables, sufficiently far from the main house to prevent discovery by Benjie and Harriet.

Sophie was pleased to see Jem again. He brought news of Seb and Dilly, and the gathering excitement about the Adversane steeplechase run. It was the talk of the county and hunting fraternity. As for Brisket, he was in fine fettle. A grand opening of the course was planned for October.

Nell was radiant at Jem's arrival, and Sophie

saw him kiss her cheeks tenderly in greeting. This young couple were in love, and she marked how the depth of their affection had withstood separation.

As she stared from her window over the shrubbery to the closed gates of Rothervale, Sophie wondered if she would ever cherish a similar commitment. She often dallied thus, speculating as to when the gates would open to admit her guardian. Some days had passed since she had seen him at Dynes Park when there had been pleasant exchanges between them. Always she recalled the memorable occasion of his intervention in the captain's room. The admiring glances of the Comte de Saint-Gabriel had emphasized her guardian's indifference; but there had been a sudden change in his demeanour when he had retained her hand and said those unforgettable words . . . *'if it be in my power to prevent, none shall take advantage of you while I am your guardian'.* Let there be no limitation, she thought, so that it will be forever in his power to prevent. She turned from the window, her excitement rising at the prospect of his arrival.

Early on the morning of the twins' birthday, Sophie visited Harriet in her room, carrying the doll's silk dress and cap. Harriet, still abed; stared open-mouthed as Sophie dressed Primrose in her new finery and fitted the matching cap upon her painted hair.

'There,' said Sophie. 'Now Primrose is ready

106

for the London salons.'

'Oh, thank you, thank you. How lovely she looks!' cried Harriet, bounding from her bed.

Sophie stooped to kiss Harriet as she placed Primrose in her arms.

'A very happy birthday, nine-year-old Harriet, and many more to come.'

She left Harriet cradling the doll and then delivered the wicker creel to Benjie. His face shone with pleasure as he examined it.

'Tomorrow it will be full of trout, I promise!'

Sophie returned to her room to complete her toilette, choosing a morning-gown of pale grey sarcenet. She selected her mother's sapphire-topped pins and, standing by the window, raised her arms to place them in her hair. She stood rigid as, at that moment, the Adversane coach wheeled in through the open gates, its two greys driven by Lord Adversane himself, standing aloft in his caped coat. After the coach had passed on its way to the carriage house, she placed the pins in her hair and lowered her arms. She stood still, staring at the gates, happy that her guardian had entered the house at last. A deep sigh escaped her when she heard Beth summoning her to the terrace.

Neither Toby nor Lord Adversane were present when Sophie arrived. Beth and governess were attempting to control the twins' exuberance as more gift parcels were opened. Paper games, a black kitten on wheels and mechanical automata were unwrapped with delight, but Sophie noticed that Harriet still clutched Primrose and yielded her only for inspection of her new gown. Fruit drinks and cakes were served and the merriment continued until the twins rushed to greet their father and uncle as they approached.

Lord Adversane stooped to embrace Benjie and Harriet, maintaining that posture to whisper to them, which produced much laughter before the twins withdrew with the governess. He turned to Sophie, who felt herself colouring as he bent graciously over her hand. Rising, he regarded her with a scintilla of amusement.

'Miss Stapleford,' he said softly, 'it behoves me as guardian to ask questions as to your wellbeing, but my eyes inform me that such enquiries are superfluous.' He paused before adding: 'You must be thankful that you didn't run away with the gypsies.'

Sophie tossed her head.

'Perhaps it is too early to judge,' she replied, with eyes twinkling.

He smiled. 'There should be a time limit.'

Returning his smile, she said: 'Set by whom, my lord?'

'By me, Miss Stapleford. The advantages of the present far outweigh those of the past. I trust you recognize the compliment I am paying you in this somewhat clumsy manner.'

'I do recognize it, my lord, and I thank you

for it; but it is to your sister that the compliment should be addressed.'

He laughed and turned to Beth. 'Miss Stapleford complains that I am lacking in my compliments to you for conferring upon her the excellent state of her wellbeing. I now do so, Beth, with apologies.'

'Nonsense, Guy. Sophie is more than capable of managing her own wellbeing and many other things besides,' said Beth, watching Toby tinkering with the mechanical automata the twins had left behind.

'Excellent,' said Guy. Turning to Sophie again, he added: 'If you could manage some wine, allow me to pour it for you, Miss Stapleford.'

'Thank you, my lord. I will so allow.'

His elegant figure turned to the wine cooler as she seated herself nearby. She had so enjoyed the good-humoured raillery with him, realizing that the sense of parity had been maintained between them.

'This confounded thing!' exploded Toby, depositing a mechanical automaton on the table beside him. 'It doesn't work properly. These little buckets should follow each other round but something jams it.'

'Benjie had it working perfectly. Leave it for him, Toby, and join us for a drink,' said Beth, setting out the chairs.

Sophie took her drink from Lord Adversane and listened to exchanges about the weather and fishing prospects for the morrow, which all viewed with favour. The mood was light, and she felt sure that Toby had yet to disclose the matter of the portfolio.

Lord Adversane moved his chair nearer to Sophie. After a glance at Beth and Toby, he said:

'Miss Stapleford, the twins have yet to receive their parents' gift of a pony and my own gift of a carriage. Would you enter into a little conspiracy with us? At this moment, the pony is being put to the carriage in the barn. You and I will try it out around the farm roads, but I would so like to see you take the first drive with Benjie and Harriet.'

Sophie flushed with pleasure. 'Of course, my lord, I shall be happy to do it. May I withdraw to change into a driving-dress?'

He nodded. 'Do so, and meet me in the barn when you are ready. Beth and Toby will do their part and arrange for the twins to be at the front porch for our arrival.'

On returning to her room, she selected a grey driving-dress, and jauntily placed a low-crown black hat over white veils which she had bound wimple-fashion around her head. Drawing on her York tan gloves, she walked along a back way to the barn, and was surprised at the hubbub. Staff were decorating the carriage with ribbons and flower garlands, directed by Jem and Nell. Lord Adversane, in his caped coat, joined Sophie in inspecting the carriage.

'It is a treasure, my lord. I have never seen anything so dainty, so fitting,' she said.

He smiled. 'I was fortunate, it was standing in Sussex. It's a pony-phaeton, ordered by Mrs Jordan for one of the Duke's children. The child must have fallen out of favour, because for some reason she changed her mind—the perils of royal patronage. The coachmaker didn't know what to do with it.'

Sophie walked round the carriage to see the pony. It was a dark-brown hackney, bred for flamboyant performance. The black leather-and-brass harness gleamed in keeping with the trappings of the pony-phaeton, now adorned with flowers.

Lord Adversane held out his hand to Sophie.

'You will accompany me, Miss Stapleford?'

Before Sophie could reply, Nell drew her aside and pinned a spray of wood-violets on her dress.

'Charming,' Lord Adversane remarked, as he leapt to the seat. He took the reins as Sophie was helped to sit beside him. 'Walk on!' he commanded, and turned to her. 'Now let's test the mettle of this little wonder.'

They proceeded slowly out of the barn, turning on to a winding lane through sun-dappled copses. Gus and Gussie joined them, unable to resist running alongside a moving carriage. Sophie relished the wonder of it, savouring the fragrant air and faint perfume from the violets on her dress. She closed her eyes and in that moment recalled her long-cherished fantasy of a carriage in motion, a lady and a gentleman, a posy and an embrace. Present circumstances bore similarities, she thought, for dreams are recalled only by fragments of reality. She had always wished herself the lady occupant, but the gallant beau had remained in the shadows. Opening her eyes, she stole a glance at Lord Adversane's countenance, handsome despite his fleeting frowns of concentration. He was the ideal, come to light from the reverie and no longer obscure. She found pleasure in watching his fine hands exercise mastery over the hackney, and realized his proximity in the confined space of the driving seat created an intimacy which increased the pounding of her heart.

His voice interposed. 'I could not permit you to take the pony without first trying him myself. Now I've put him through his paces, I feel certain you'll handle him with competence, so be assured, Miss Stapleford.'

She forced herself to reply. 'He answers well, my lord.'

So they continued, he inviting her approbation and responding delightedly to her admiration of the equipage. At last they arrived at the open main gates of Rothervale, and turned down the drive to the porch. It had ended all too soon. She wished the drive could have continued for miles.

As they approached the porch, applause could be heard from where Beth and Toby stood with the twins, the governess and other staff. Coming to a halt, they were surrounded by all, praising the decorated carriage and handsome pony. Benjie and Harriet jumped up and down with joy.

Lord Adversane handed the reins to Sophie, and lit down to help seat Benjie and Harriet beside her. Everyone watched as Sophie proceeded to the park gates, where she turned the carriage and allowed Benjie to drive back. Then it was Harriet's turn, and so was passed a pleasant afternoon with Sophie grateful for the levelling effect of the twins' company. After helping to install the pony-phaeton in the carriage house, she dashed upstairs to change into her favourite French cambric gown.

Tea-time was shared with all members of the family. Cakes, lemonade, sugared fruits and sweetmeats were served. Benjie showed off his new creel and Harriet introduced the now fashionable Primrose. After puzzle games set by Toby, the lively blindman's-buff and hunt-the-slipper meant that urgings to bed were immediately obeyed by the twins.

The exhausted adults sought refuge in enjoying what promised to be a spectacular sunset. Sophie stood by the balustrade, gazing over the gardens, happy with the day's events. There was no breeze, only stillness and a roseate glow from the ever-changing sky. She was joined by Lord Adversane carrying two glasses of wine. He offered one to her and she took it with a smile.

They sipped in silence, he regarding her over the rim of his glass.

'Have you yet been approached by Barty Wardyne, Miss Stapleford?' he asked.

'No, my lord. I do not expect to hear from him since his recall to duty was due at any moment.'

A pause ensued, before he spoke again.

'In time, on your return to the manor house, you must try the Adversane steeplechase.'

'Oh, yes,' she enthused. 'Sir Toby has told me of it and I hear it's the talk of the county.'

'It presents excellent sport, and work is proceeding on it for a grand opening at the beginning of October.'

'I shall look forward to that, my lord.'

'As will I, Miss Stapleford. As will I,' he replied, happily.

She wondered whether to broach the matter of Hallam in this exclusive moment, but she deferred. Supper was imminent and, on finishing their drinks, he offered his arm to escort her to the dining-room.

'A red sky at night is the shepherd's delight,' he intoned as they walked along the terrace.

'I have heard the rhyme said as "the sailor's delight",' rejoined Sophie.

He smiled, looking down at her. 'Perhaps

the sailor's daughter's delight?'

'That cannot be relied upon until the sailor is home,' she said quietly.

He halted and faced her. Lowering his voice, he said:

'I am in touch with a naval friend of mine, Lieutenant Jack Watts, who has secret contacts in France. Your father is moved frequently by his captors, as they suspect a rescue may be mounted. I do not wish to raise your hopes unnecessarily, Miss Stapleford, but I repose confidence in the Admiralty's doing all they can to secure your father's release. It is always in my mind.'

She nodded, whispering 'Thank you', finding difficulty in saying more.

During the meal Toby mentioned Mrs Lachbone's paintings.

'You have Sophie to thank for procuring and safeguarding 'em. I think it right that she joins us later in the library where I have the portfolio under lock and key.'

Lord Adversane was immediately interested. He voiced a wish to go to the library at once, but was persuaded to curb his impatience until the meal was over. Once in the library, he sat silently studying each painting for some time until curtains were drawn and candelabra lit. He stirred, nodding thoughtfully. He turned to Sophie.

'I am most grateful, Miss Stapleford,' he said. 'With your permission, I should like to lodge the portfolio with Sir Henry Nancarrow, as the paintings are likely to be a chief element in the claim.'

'It would make Mrs Lachbone very happy if you could use them for that purpose,' said Sophie, 'though I should emphasize, my lord, that Mr Hallam is intent on finding and destroying them. I mention this purely as a caution.'

Lord Adversane shook his head, his eyes hard and bright.

'Have no fear, Miss Stapleford, I shall guard them with my life. Keep them locked up, Toby, until I leave.'

There was a silence. Then Sophie spoke.

'Please assure me, my lord, that you will not grant permission for Mr Hallam to occupy the manor house.'

Lord Adversane looked stunned by her request.

'How did this arise?'

'He called at the manor house as I was on the point of leaving. He objected to Mr and Mrs Parker being appointed custodians during my absence.'

Lord Adversane rose, crossed to the chimney-breast and stood for a moment, his face flushed.

'Mr Hallam has no right to enter the manor house, let alone occupy it,' he said firmly. 'I shall visit Mr and Mrs Parker as soon as possible to make sure they have not been importuned by him.'

Sophie, reassured by this forthright answer, then regretted raising the matter as it appeared to affect his lordship's disposition. He returned to the open portfolio, fingering its contents in a frowning silence. Toby joined him at the table.

'This Hallam's a scoundrel. You should hasten to Sir Henry and put your case. Who knows what the man will do next?'

'I shall send a letter by courier to Sir Henry seeking an urgent appointment with him.'

'The sooner, the better,' muttered Toby.

Sophie rose from her chair and quietly withdrew, leaving the two gentlemen earnestly conversing.

The house was quiet. Beth had probably retired by now. After the excitements of the day, with the promise of more on the morrow, Sophie decided to seek her bed and took a candle from the hall table to light her way upstairs. She sighed with relief that at last the portfolio was in Lord Adversane's hands. More than this, she rejoiced in those special intimacies with her guardian and knew that across her pillow would flow dreamings of incipient tenderness for him.

It was some time before Guy realized Sophie had slipped away unobserved.

'Demme, Toby! Did you see her leave?'

'No, but I'm not surprised. She is sensitive of her situation here and feels she intrudes. It's an example of her innate good manners.'

'I was about to ask her to share a posset with us.'

'She's probably retired to her room.' Guy whipped round expectantly as the library door opened to admit Beth. 'I thought you were Sophie returned,' he said.

'I waited until I was sure Sophie had left you,' said Beth. 'This letter arrived by courier earlier and its enclosure presents a dilemma.'

'In what way?' asked Toby.

Beth held up a sealed envelope. 'This is addressed to "Miss Sophia Stapleford by kind favour of the Lady Elizabeth Dallimore".'

'That is in order, Beth,' said Guy. 'You simply pass it on to her.'

'That was my first intention, but then—well, you are her guardian, Guy.'

He smiled. 'I am unaware of Miss Stapleford's likely correspondents. Who is the sender of the covering letter?'

'The covering letter is not unexpected but it has arrived sooner than I thought. It is the identity of the writer that causes the dilemma.'

'And the writer is?' Guy asked.

'The Comte de Saint-Gabriel.'

'Anton!' exclaimed Guy, reaching for the letter. He looked at the envelope, at the well-known hand of his friend. 'There only one reason that qualifies him to address Miss Stapleford,' he said quietly, 'and that is to apologize for his atrocious behaviour at the manor house.'

'So you agree that I should hand it to Sophie tomorrow morning? I could not do so without your knowledge, Guy,' said Beth.

Guy hesitated, then returned the letter to Beth.

'I'm sure it contains nothing controversial, but grant Miss Stapleford the option to tell us should she find the contents offensive in any way.'

'For what reason was the *comte* writing to you in the first place, my dear?' asked Toby.

'When I met him during my visit to Adversane, I told him of our wish to refurbish the games gallery at Rothervale. He offered help in measuring the fencing-pistes. His letter says he would be free to visit in a month or so.'

Guy sank into a chair with a groan. 'Anton coming here? To stay? That puts a different complexion on it. Could you put him off, Beth?'

Beth closed her eyes and took a deep breath.

'I have good reason to make the attempt. The Italian music-tutor will be here within a day or so and shall remain with us for several weeks. Should Anton come during that time, my task as Sophie's chaperon will be hugely complicated. It is not an ideal situation.'

There was an uneasy silence. Then Guy spoke.

'What about that posset? I think we could all benefit from one.'

Toby summoned a footman as Guy stretched out his booted legs and clasped his hands behind his head. He watched Beth seat herself and place the letters on a table by her chair. There was high colour in her cheeks and her fingers hovered over the letters, fitfully tapping them.

'You are upset, Beth,' said Guy gently. 'Anton must be dissuaded. I shall write to him immediately and insist upon it.' Beth nodded her head in agreement.

Further comment lapsed as a footman entered and served the possets. They sipped in silence.

Guy, more concerned than he cared to show, decided there and then to visit Rothervale more frequently. Beth might need his assistance in entertaining these two gentlemen as house guests, should their visits coincide. There was also the possibility that Barty Wardyne might come to call.

'That will be a pretty kettle of fish,' he said, thinking aloud. 'That's what we hope tomorrow's picnic will yield,' said Toby. 'A pretty kettle of fish.'

CHAPTER SEVEN

Sophie lay in bed, her eyes half-closed and a hand reaching out to stroke the silky ears of Gussie, sitting beside the bed on the powder-robe. Morning sun bathed the room in golden light and through the window Sophie could see an azure sky. This augured well for the fishing picnic.

She had slept fitfully, wishing she had not asked the question that so affected her guardian. She could not withdraw it and determined the coming day would pass without mentioning Mr Hallam's name.

She rose as Nell entered with hot water and towels.

'It's a beautiful morning, Miss Sophie. Everyone says it's going to be a scorcher. Would you wish me to lay out a lighter gown for you?'

Why not, thought Sophie.

'I'll wear the gossamer white, Nell, with my grey spencer and half-boots to match.'

'And a straw bonnet?'

'Yes, the white-ribboned one,' said Sophie, entering the wash-closet.

She felt at fault in airing her minor issue when his lordship had an abundance of his own, and regretted leaving the library so summarily without an assurance of the trust she reposed in him.

Her toilette completed, a hesitant knock on the door caused her to turn.

'Come in,' she called, and was surprised to see Beth already dressed for the picnic.

'Sophie, I shall make my way down to the picnic site, near the fallen sycamore. Join us there as soon as you are ready. Guy and Toby are gone up-river, but a young gentleman awaits you to teach him to cast a line properly.'

Sophie smiled. 'Tell him to make sure his creel is nearby. All I have to do is tidy my hair and tie my bonnet.'

'It becomes you, Sophie, and how lovely you look in white!' Beth paused, and drew something from her reticule. 'I have received a letter from the Comte de Saint-Gabriel with which he enclosed another for me to pass to you. Guy is willing for you to have it as he is sure it contains an apology. If, though, there is anything in the letter that offends you, please be sure to tell us.'

Sophie felt herself blushing.

'How surprising,' she murmured, taking the letter from Beth's hand. 'I shall read it later.'

'You do not have to hasten to the picnic, Sophie. We are by no means ready so you will have time to read your letter.'

'I had thought to help you.'

'All is in hand; but if you could keep an eye on Benjie and Harriet, that is of prime importance to my peace of mind. Sophie, do read your letter first,' said Beth as she left.

Sophie stared at the envelope for some moments before she opened it and started to read.

Lord Adversane was right in his assumption that the *comte*'s letter contained an apology for his presumptuous gallantry on first meeting. It was genuinely expressed, Sophie thought, and unnecessary in reality. The *comte*'s part in the incident had become a triviality to her and, far from offending had earned him a modicum of gratitude, for it provoked her guardian and drove away his indifference to her. Even now, remembering his intervention gave her pleasure.

She sighed and passed to the second page of the letter. The sentences that followed caused her to sit dazedly on her bed.

Her heart pounded and her cheeks burned as she read:

. . . When shall you release Lord Adversane from your affairs so that he is able to return to London? He has been so long away from a certain young lady who pines for him and writes him daily. His attentions to you cause her distress and she imagines her hopes at risk. It would please her if you could lighten his burdens and persuade him to return with all speed. Chère mademoiselle, *perhaps you should find a husband to protect and maintain you so*

that our monseigneur may pursue his own desires. Vraiment *he has voiced such concerns to me . . .*

Profoundly offended, she could read no more and tossed the letter aside. It fell to the floor, where she left it.

For a moment she remained, endeavouring to calm herself, then rose and crossed to the mirror. While deciding to join the picnic, she studied her face. She must control her features to convey that the *comte's* letter was of little consequence; but there was a phrase which rankled: ' . . . *he has voiced such concerns to me . . .*' This implied she had been the subject of complaint by Lord Adversane! Could this be so? Was her informant credible? She wished to give her guardian the benefit of the doubt, and determined her disillusion would be cloaked by felicity.

She pinned up her hair, which had grown since Dilly clipped it, and tied on her bonnet. She paused for a moment composing herself, before leaving to join the family.

She had recently explored the fishing-grounds, a deep back-water of the river to the east of the house. Meadows sloped down to its shores, but at the top of the hill was a folly, a stone Ionic temple, built as a ruin by a seventeenth century forebear of Sir Toby.

It seemed that everyone had gathered by the river. She was alone. She passed the creepered crevices of the folly and continued downhill through sunswept meadows with drifts of wine-red sorrel and multitudes of buttercups. Swinging her reticule, she viewed with illogical charm the yellow pollen deposited on her gown as she progressed. Continuous birdsong came from a little copse, and lifted her spirits. It really was going to be a beautiful day.

By the fallen sycamore near the river, white cloths were spread on which were pies, mutton-chops, cold fowl, crusty bread, mead and lardy-cakes. Boxes of cutlery alternated with stacked platters amid flagons of wine and ale. House staff and old retainers were invited, bringing rods for themselves.

Some distance from the picnic site, Beth had spread a blanket and beckoned Sophie to join her.

'How lovely this is,' breathed Sophie. 'Where are the others?'

'Toby and Guy are still upstream. But Benjie has been looking for you. He is disappointed he has only one fly.'

'That should be sufficient for our purpose,' said Sophie. 'Where is he now?'

'Taking some refreshment with Harriet.'

'I will go and find them,' said Sophie, leaving her bonnet and reticule in Beth's care.

'Won't you eat first, Sophie? There's a sufficiency of food.'

'No, thank you, Beth. I have no appetite for

125

it.'

'The letter, Sophie. It was acceptable?'

'As was supposed, it contained an apology but nothing else of moment.'

She rose, as Benjie and Harriet came running towards them.

'I've only one fly, Sophie,' gasped Benjie.

'Let me see it,' said Sophie. Benjie brought it from his creel. 'Light mallard feather wings; very suitable, Benjie. Let's find a place downstream with space for you to cast.'

Benjie handed his rod and line to Sophie and took up his creel. Harriet, hugging Primrose in her new finery, followed them to the water's edge, and on downstream until Sophie halted.

'Do you see that flow in the river, passing the shadow of the overhanging bank on the other side, Benjie?' asked Sophie.

Benjie nodded. 'There's a trout there.'

'Probably facing upstream and waiting for your fly. Now we want the fly to float towards him to his side of that flow, looking as tempting to him as a sugar-plum is to you.'

By this time, Sophie had taken his rod and pulled enough line to cover the distance between Benjie and his trout. With the fly and hook set, she said:

'Hold the line, cast the fly in that flow and slowly let the line out. Do not jerk it—gently let it drift . . .'

Benjie's first cast fell short and he tried

again. Sophie and Harriet watched him cast many times until suddenly, the line became taut and Benjie struggled with a trout as it lunged and dived. Encouraged by shouts from Sophie and Harriet, he eventually landed it.

'A worthwhile catch! Not far short of a pound and a half,' said Sophie, as he placed the trout in his creel.

Harriet, in bending low over the creel to inspect the trout, was accidentally prodded by Benjie's elbow as he was drawing out the line. She teetered on the bank and, losing her balance, fell into the shallows and released her hold on Primrose. The doll, caught by the flow, slowly drifted Ophelia-like downstream, surrounded by trailing waterweeds. Harriet screamed, not for her own plight, but for Primrose, whose petticoats were now floating around her head exposing her entire construction.

Sophie helped the wailing Harriet out of the water.

'Primrose, Primrose,' sobbed the child.

Relieving the stunned Benjie of his rod, Sophie removed her half-boots and stepped into the shallows. Eyeing the distance to the bobbing Primrose, she waded deeper, checked the fly and hook, and cast the line. It floated aloft, descended near the doll, catching on one of the flounces of the dress she had stitched. The current tugged, set the hook, and she started to reel in until she brought the doll into the shallows. She reached out, just as her foot sank into a hole, tipping her headlong into the water as she tossed the doll towards a clump of irises.

Benjie waded in and removed the hook. He presented Harriet with Primrose, her petticoats saturated, the yellow-silk dress torn and her cap vanished in the flow.

Sophie, handing Benjie his rod once more, climbed out of the water and sat on the bank. Mollified by the rescue, Harriet pounced on her, hugging her in gratitude.

At that moment Beth appeared, and listened with concern to the recounting of the incident by Benjie and Harriet. Sophie reassured her, suggesting that Harriet be properly dried off at the house.

'You, too, must return to the house, Sophie, to change all your clothes. You are far wetter than Harriet so do not delay,' said Beth, as she left with the children.

Sophie stared dejectedly at the river for some moments, then regarded with dismay the effect of the water on her dress and hose. She took up her half-boots, rose from the bank, and gasped at the muddy soiling. The day had belied its promise.

She walked to the top of the hill, exuding water-drops, and sat on the steps of the folly, where she dried off her feet as best she could and put on the half-boots. Her hair, which had become unpinned, fell into her eyes. She held it back with both hands clasped to her temples. A simmering irritability intensified at the sight of her spoiled dress and an intrusive wetness everywhere on her person.

Suddenly, she was startled by a footfall and, looking over her shoulder, saw her guardian approaching with a blanket over his arm. She rose and, turning away from him, retreated into an embrasure.

'Miss Stapleford, Sophie!'

'I am in no mood to be seen or spoken with . . .'

'You are our heroine of the day. We came back and Beth told us what had happened. Come, you need this blanket after your wetting.'

He came towards her and placed the blanket over her shoulders. 'I think you should join Harriet at the house and share her hot drinks,' he continued gently.

For a moment she remained with head bowed, draped in the blanket. Then she looked up, her eyes bright with challenge.

'I'm sorry you have had to spoil your fishing attending to me, my lord. It is an aspect of your guardianship you must find tiresome indeed.'

'I do not find it tiresome at all,' he protested.

Ignoring his remark, she continued: 'There is no need to delay your return to London on my account. The young lady who pines for you and writes to you daily cannot lay the blame upon me for distracting you, my lord.'

He was dumbfounded. 'What do you mean?' Then, recovering he added: 'It is necessary for me to visit London on matters about Adversane and, at thc same time, I intend to see Jack Watts concerning your father, but I do not wish to remain there. As for this young lady, I would be pleased to know who she is and why she addresses daily outpourings to me?'

'Perhaps she is one of your jilted females!' She stepped back, placing a hand over her mouth, as if regretting her rejoinder. He stared at her in disbelief, slowly shaking his head.

'What is the source of this rubbish?'

She did not answer and bowed her head.

'You have recently received a letter from that fount of gossip and scandal, the Comte de Saint-Gabriel. Is it to him I owe this outburst?'

She looked up. 'You should not be surprised, for he claims you have voiced these concerns to him, and . . .'

'Do you think for one moment I discuss such things with others?' he interposed. His voice was hard.

'And . . . and . . .' she gulped, her eyes brimming, 'you wish me to find a husband so that you may be free of your responsibilities!'

He was shocked at this and took a step towards her. His voice softened.

'As for a husband, I have said from the

outset that I will not consider an offer from anyone, however suitable to your position, while you are my ward. Matters affecting your future are for your father to decide, certainly not for a guardian in circumstances of limited tenure.'

She covered her face with her hands.

Guy saw the locks of hair fallen around her face, and her stained dress under the dark picnic blanket. She looked forsaken, as when first he saw her. Holding the folds of the blanket, he drew her slowly to him. His arm closed around her, and with his free hand he gently held her head against his shoulder. Unresisting, she nestled against him.

She was like a bewildered child, he thought. Yet, was she a child? The damp dress clung to her in those places where the eye should not linger, revealing her as a young woman, a very desirable one! He held her closer and raised her face, smiling down at her.

'Sophie, do you think I should call Anton out for upsetting you by his untruths?'

'On no account. I should not have misjudged you.'

He lightly kissed her temples and cheeks then passed his lips softly over hers.

'I shall hurry back from London and will come straightway to you at Rothervale,' he whispered.

'Oh, you will come directly to Rothervale?'

'How could I do otherwise?'

'With news of my dear father, I trust!'

Her dear father! A sudden tension caused him to release her. These words struck him as blows. His advances rendered his guardianship less than exemplary. He had taken advantage of his ward's vulnerability and he must never do so again. It was not honourable, for honour imposes restraint. The loss of honour would make it impossible to sustain his self-esteem and to face Captain Sir John Stapleford.

He stepped back. 'Come,' he said evenly, offering his hand. 'I shall take you back to the house.'

After picking up her sodden hose and clutching the blanket around her, she took his hand. Affected by what had passed between them, they walked in silence together until, at the terrace steps, he halted.

'I shall leave you here, Miss Stapleford. I apologize for what has happened. As your guardian, I wish to act correctly in every respect.'

'There is no cause for you to apologize, my lord. You have relieved my mind on the *comte*'s claims.'

He released her hand then strode across the lawns towards the fishing-grounds. After some distance, he turned.

'It's the very devil being your guardian!' he shouted. His words were wasted on the empty terrace as Sophie had already entered the house.

Guy picked up a stick with which he whipped the longer grasses as he walked. Bewilderment surged in his mind. Young ladies he had courted in the past seldom matched his own desires. He was convinced he would never find a life companion who could be as content in the country as in London salons. Could it be that his ward might fulfil that ideal? Her beauty and poise were without question, her refinement and grace all he could wish. He admired her prowess at riding and driving, and now fly-fishing. More than this, she had spirit and intelligence, and had cast a spell over the Dallimores.

He thought he should visit Rothervale less frequently and allow Sophie to continue under Beth's wing without the possibility of romantic dalliance. However, there were the other gentlemen to consider; but for himself, honour imposed a barrier to any hopes he might have so far as his ward was concerned. It would remain so until the captain returned. He flung the stick into a ditch. It was perplexing and damnable.

In her room, Sophie removed her stained dress so that Nell could take it to the laundry-maids. Her room was redolent of the sweet river smell, reminding her of the doll's rescue and her guardian's tenderness. She had admired him from the instant she met him, and her regard had heightened on every subsequent occasion. To him was due her new-found confidence. It gave her pleasure to watch him and be near him. Joy flooded when she thought of his embrace, his kisses and assurances. He had called her 'Sophie' for the first time.

She selected a light lavender gown and, tidying her hair, prepared to join the picnic once more. Before doing so, she peeped into Harriet's room. Harriet was fast asleep, cuddling Primrose, who wore once more the gingham dress and apron.

Sophie smiled to herself. Like Primrose she had been caught in a strong current. Unlike Primrose, who had escaped it, Sophie felt drawn in an undertow from which escape was impossible. Submission implied no weakness but a docile drift toward discovery. A degree of intimacy had occurred with her guardian. Nothing concerning him would ever be quite the same again.

CHAPTER EIGHT

Sleep eluded Guy that night in his comfortable apartment at Rothervale. A bedside candle still burned, and he lay back staring at the crimson damask of the tester. Tomorrow promised to be a day of departures.

He rose, slipped into a dressing-robe and drew back the window-curtains. The night was dark but a clouded moon gave a diffused light which made the trees appear spectral, their grotesque shapes wavering to his eye. He closed the curtains, dug his hands in his pockets and paced the room.

He did not wish to delay his return to Adversane, and from there prepare for a London visit to see Sir Henry, taking with him the precious portfolio, safely packed in a leather satchel provided by Toby. The paintings added substance to his claim. 'Sophie, how well you serve my cause,' he murmured, 'and how little I deserve it.'

He was reluctant to face his ward and judged himself harshly for his advances to her. Her plight and childlike demeanour commanded sympathy and protection. Although his initial moves were driven by such paternal feelings, he was all too soon aware of their displacement. He grimaced as he recalled his promise to her '. . . *none shall take advantage of you while I am your guardian . . .*' In truth, his own vulnerability had been tested and found wanting.

In the dim light, he stopped to regard an early portrait of his father which was set over the chimney-piece. He knew it well and needed no extra illumination to read the words *Cautus et Audax* scrolled in gold at the top left hand side of the painting. It was the family motto: 'Cautious and Bold'. He bowed his head. 'Timely advice, my dear sir,' he whispered. His gallantry with Sophie had landed him on the edge of a precipice, and drawing back, he resolved to maintain a polite distance in future dealings with his ward. Caution he would observe; boldness must bide in the shadows for now.

He settled on top of the bed and drowsed for some brief moments. As soon as the first glimmer of morning light broke through a chink in the curtains, he rose and summoned Lewis, his valet.

After taking breakfast in his room, he dressed for driving and, carrying the leather satchel, left for the carriage house to ensure that all was ready. Satisfied, he distributed vails to the grooms before returning to the house to take his leave. He found Beth and Toby at breakfast in the dining-room, but Sophie was nowhere to be seen.

Beth raised her eyebrows on noting he was ready for travel.

'Won't you join us, Guy?' she asked.

'I have taken breakfast in my room, Beth, and am now anxious to leave.' He stooped to kiss her. 'A most enjoyable sojourn, as usual.'

Toby rose and extended his hand. 'I see you have the portfolio. Keep it safe, Guy. Call on me at St Stephen's when you arrive in London.'

'I will, Toby. I'd like you to come with me to Sir Henry's chambers when I present the portfolio.'

'Of course, dear boy. You can count on it.'

Guy released Toby's hand and turned towards the door.

'You are in haste, Guy,' said Beth. 'Why so?'

'I intend to see the Parkers at the manor house on my way back. Then I must write a letter of dismissal to Hynde Hallam before I leave for London. All this may take time.'

He could not reveal that he wished to avoid Sophie, but Beth unwittingly reassured him with the comment:

'Sophie will be disappointed not to see you before you go. She's out on an early ride.'

Chasing dreams again, he thought.

His coach was waiting by the porch, his footman, groom and valet already seated. Guy leapt to the box, took up the reins and was soon away, out of the front gates and on the road to Adversane. Morning mists hovered in drifts, which caused Guy to slow down since farm wagons were abroad at this hour and cattle were on the move. A large herd surrounded Guy's coach and a carriage approached from the other direction, halting their progress. Guy called to the cowman to drive the herd to the swards at the roadside; slowly the road cleared. The carriage came to a halt beside Guy, and a young gentleman leaned from its window. He doffed an elegant buckled hat, revealing fair hair lying in waves, and smiled.

'We are not sure whether we are on the

right road for the house of Sir Tobias Dallimore. Do you know of it, good sir?'

'You are nearby,' said Guy. 'Some three miles will take you to the gates on your right. Is that your destination?'

'It is, good sir. I am a *musicista* and have been granted the honour to instruct his children in those arts.'

Guy nodded, waiting as the gentleman withdrew to his seat and the carriage moved forward. He frowned. He had not expected the Italian music-tutor, engaged by Beth, to be so youthsome and well-favoured, nor that he would speak impeccable English. Although reposing confidence in Beth's judgement, Guy was not entirely comfortable that the *signor* was to stay in such close proximity to his ward. Then, he thought, country girl that she is, Sophie was unlikely to show the remotest interest in music.

He was not enjoying the drive back. He slowed to a walking-pace but his mind raced with speculation. Why had he thought that Sophie would not be interested in music? His presumption simply expressed his hope, and marked how little he knew her. He shook his head sadly, now regretting his precipitate departure without bidding her farewell.

*   *   *

After her ride that morning, Sophie was not

surprised to learn that Lord Adversane had left Rothervale. Yesterday, when she returned to the picnic after her dousing, she had hoped his conciliatory demeanour toward her would continue; but this was not to be. He had distanced himself, with apologies. She so wished to persuade him that his attendance on her at the folly had been appropriate to the circumstances, certainly no more and no less than the consolation she would have expected from her father. There was not a moment her guardian spared for her and, in attempting to engage him, she met with cold indifference.

Seated at the dressing-table, she tusselled with her hair. Using two brushes to smooth out the tangles, her eyes brimmed. When would she hear some news of her father? Could she rely on her guardian to pursue the matter with urgency, when he afforded little opportunity for her to express her fears? She sighed, pinning up her hair.

She missed Nell, who was preparing to return to Adversane that day, taking with her Sophie's river-spoiled dress for repair by Dilly. Nell would be away for a week, at least. Also, Sir Toby's journey to London loomed, if not today then surely tomorrow. The regime of the house would change in favour of gentler domestic pursuits.

That being so, Sophie thought to while away the time stitching another frock for Primrose. Leaving the dressing-table, she looked down as a soft wet nose nuzzled her hand. 'Dear Gussie,' she murmured, 'you always cheer me when my spirits are low.' She stooped to hug and frisk with her before going downstairs.

It was on the landing she first heard it. The most glorious piano music resounded through the house. She drew breath as, captivated, she descended the stairs. The salon doors were wide open. She stood at the threshold, unable to take her eyes from the broad-shouldered pianist striking the keys to perfection, and charming utterly the little group gathered near him. The pianist toyed and hesitated, fetching romantic artistry from the notes. The power of the music and its sheer beauty touched her, until latent tears flowed unashamedly. The piece ended, its last note floating into silence. A spontaneous sigh of pleasure and admiration from all present preceded the vigorous clapping of hands. Sophie groped in her reticule for a kerchief, and dabbed her eyes.

Beth approached, holding out her hand.

'Come and meet Signor Bordoni, Sophie. He has just arrived and is trying out the Broadwood.'

The *signor* rose, stepped forward and stood deferentially on the red-carpeted floor in a yellow square of sunlight. Sir Toby effected the introductions, whereupon *the signor* bent over Sophie's hand.

'*Che bella!*' he whispered, his sparkling dark

eyes engaging her.

In that instant, she was aware of a strange overwhelming attraction, and knew that the weeks to come would offer more entrancing pursuits than the making of dolls' clothes.

He smiled, indicating her kerchief.

'My playing has made you cry?'

She nodded.

'It was lacking?'

She laughed. 'Oh no, it was wonderful. What was the piece you selected to play?'

'It was the *allegro assai* from a piano sonata by van Beethoven, known as the *Apassionata.*

'This is the first time I have heard it. I shall never forget it,' she said.

Still smiling, he inclined his head in acknowledgment.

A footman approached, and Beth gave instructions to escort the *signor* to the apartment prepared for him. As he left the salon, Signor Bordoni playfully beckoned to Benjie and Harriet to join him. Both rushed to do so, eager to befriend their charming new tutor.

'He is a treasure,' said Sophie dreamily.

'I hear nothing but praise from all the houses in which he has stayed. His mother is English and his father an Italian maestro, both still active in opera in London,' said Beth. 'Before he leaves, we shall arrange a musical evening. The signor has three friends who will grace the occasion to make up a quartet.'

Toby smiled approval. 'If you let me know in good time, I'll be sure to be here. In fact, I might bring a guest or two. How long will he be staying?'

'No longer than six weeks,' said Beth. 'He has other appointments to keep.'

'I'll plan accordingly,' Toby replied. Then, turning to Sophie, he added: 'Do you think you could drive me to Horsham, Sophie? It's not too far and I could pick up the London coach from there. We'll take a groom in case of mishap. Beth thought you'd enjoy the brief excursion.'

Sophie brightened. 'Of course, Toby.'

'Tomorrow morning, then. Crack o' dawn!'

Later, after an evening repast, Sophie joined Beth, Toby and Signor Bordoni on the terrace, where dessert wines and sweet-meats were served. At Toby's prompting, the *signor* regaled them with stories of Italian opera and the grand palaces in which generations of his family had performed in Italy.

'But my own branch of the family,' he continued, 'has made London its home since the early eighteenth century, performing by the royal command of both Queen Anne and King George I. *Londra e diventata la mia casa.*'

He spoke with many a graceful gesture of his hands and the inclusion of the occasional Italian phrase added to the charm of his discourse.

'We are aware that you are a singer, but do

you play other instruments as well as the piano?' asked Beth.

'I have a penchant for the violin, and enjoy composing simple pieces for the piano, songs and such. Sometimes I conclude a visiting tutorial with a little song about my pupils, so you must warn Master Benjie and Miss Harriet to be on their best behaviour.'

'I think that our Miss Sophie could assist you,' said Toby. 'Unbeknown to her, I have listened to the most competent playing in the salon at times . . .'

'Oh no, I have no real talent . . .' protested Sophie, feeling a deep flush spreading over her cheeks.

'And,' added Beth, 'she has a sweet singing voice.'

The *signor* turned to Sophie. 'You must join our sessions. Please consent, Miss Sophia.'

He had used her full name, with an emphasis on the second syllable, 'Miss Soph-*ee*-ah'. Spoken thus, she had to admit the *signor* possessed a talent to transform the ordinary into something extraordinary.

'I have much to learn from you,' she said.

Candleshine through the windows fell across the terrace as dusk approached. Beth rose.

'Let us go inside. Perhaps Signor Bordoni would treat us to more of his excellent playing before we retire.'

The *signor* did not hesitate. As Toby and

Beth seated themselves, he opened the piano. Sophie stood nearby, watching his competent fingers produce chords and scales which echoed round the salon. After a moment, he paused, and seriously regarded her.

'A song, perhaps?' he asked.

She nodded, smiling.

'What is your pleasure, Miss Sophia?'

'It must be your choice, surely,' she replied.

He smiled, engaging her eyes. 'Then I will select Handel's *Silent Worship.*'

'I do not know that song,' she said.

'You could have inspired it.'

He lowered his eyes to the keyboard, played the introduction and began to sing in a mellifluous tenor voice. Sophie stood enchanted by the words of the quatrains and the emotions they summoned. All too soon, the song ended:

> '*Surely you heard my lady*
> *Out in the garden there,*
> *Rivalling the glitt'ring sunshine*
> *With the glory of golden hair.*'

His hands rested upon the piano keys as he looked up at her.

'Not so silent a worship, for the lyrics are beautiful,' she whispered.

'You really could have inspired them, Miss Sophia,' he answered.

All applauded, and other songs followed. As

the recital proceeded, Sophie warmed to the *signor.* It is said that eyes are windows to the soul, and she had seen courtesy and kindliness in his. His glances were neither furtive nor optative, but admiring and respectful. A shared love of music augured that nothing but good could come of their meeting.

That night, Sophie prepared her driving-dress for the morrow. She lay in bed and sighed contentedly. Her sadness had vanished, as had the uncharitable thoughts about Lord Adversane. Observing deep-felt principles forced him to tread a path strewn with difficulties. While admiring his strength of purpose, she longed for him to be free to follow his own will, and thought of him with affectionate concern.

The next morning, though misty, promised well. After a light breakfast, Sophie joined Beth in the hall, watching Toby as he directed the loading of his phaeton. Sophie noted his portly figure was dressed for London, elegant in a new black redingote and hessians.

After bidding Beth farewell, Sophie left to mount the phaeton. With the groom's help she settled herself to drive, and took up the reins as Toby approached and climbed up beside her. With a last wave to Beth she brought the hackney to order and soon they were on their way to Five Oaks.

The road was rutted and rough, and Sophie was cautious as to speed.

'It gets better beyond Billingshurst,' said Toby.

The chalk hills were robed in flowers rejoicing in the risen sun.

'That wide-open yellow goatsbeard is telling us we're early starters,' said Sophie, indicating a roadside bloom. 'Its popular name is "Jack-go-to-bed-at-Noon". It's always closed before midday.'

'That's why I've never seen it,' said Toby. 'You must notice these things on those early morning rides you take. Why do you do that, Sophie?'

'It's an escape from reality.'

'Is reality so dreadful?'

There was a long pause before she answered.

'I am concerned for my father.'

'Guy is pursuing that matter. He views it as of great importance.'

'He is anxious to be relieved of me.'

'On the contrary, he enjoys the attachment. He admires your courage and feels he falls short in his guardianship. Only your father's return could achieve your supreme happiness. With that in mind he is determined to sustain his contact with the Admiralty.' There was a long silence. Then Toby added gruffly: 'Guy's own position is precarious. He has the devil and all to pay and his misfortunes are rife. I fear for him and for Adversane.'

Sophie frowned. 'Are your fears founded on

146

his claim against Hallam and . . .' Sophie broke off as the phaeton hit a large stone and rocked violently. She managed to steady it, as Toby continued:

'Guy is not aware of Hallam's associates. I believe they are part of a clique run by a notorious criminal from the Seven Dials. Gabe Driscoll employs the latter syllable of his surname as a nickname with a threat in it— The Skull. His visage resembles one, I'm told—yellow veined skin stretched tightly over prominent cheekbones—lips set in a permanent grin. Guy will be out of his depth if I'm proved right.'

Sophie's heart plummeted. She could not bear to think of Lord Adversane threatened by Hallam and his ilk. 'What can be done?' she asked.

'We shall have to muster our patience until Guy sees Sir Henry,' said Toby with a grimace.

Sophie turned the phaeton on to the Horsham Road. It was less stony and they picked up speed.

'I'm grateful that you have confided Lord Adversane's plight to me, Toby,' she said. 'It explains many things.'

'That was my intention,' Toby replied.

She glanced at his smiling face, which hinted that he had planned this drive for the purpose of such revelations.

The town was well awake and every thoroughfare was crowded with carriages and people. Sophie drove through the arch to the yard of the King's Head. The groom took the reins and Toby tipped an ostler to attend to the horse. Sophie hitched up her driving-dress and accompanied Toby into the inn for a short respite before starting the return journey.

A group of prosperous-looking gentlemen surrounded Toby.

'Constituent businessmen,' he whispered to Sophie, 'all wanting favours.' They stepped back, allowing Toby to escort Sophie to a window-seat, where he ordered coffee and ratafia for her. 'Bear with me, Sophie,' he said softly. 'I shall quickly dismiss these people.' He rejoined his constituent group, and dealt summarily with them, brushing aside many a leering nod and wink raised by Sophie's presence.

She ignored the badinage. Her thoughts were with her guardian. It was inconceivable that Adversane might be lost should his claim fail. If that happened, the manor house would have to be surrendered. Where would her father go when released? She shuddered at the thought of Hallam occupying the manor house. Neither could she tolerate the thought of that man with the horrible name, The Skull, strutting about and plundering the Adversane estate.

Such a calamity must be averted. She vowed there and then to aid Lord Adversane in this challenge and do all that the situation demanded of her. The sense of commitment invigorated her. She sighed deeply. A long-travelled road had at last led her to a worthy destination.

CHAPTER NINE

The days settled into an idyllic routine. Sophie joined the morning music-lesson in the salon, and sat quietly stitching a new frock for Primrose. She enjoyed the *signor*'s lively stories of the composers and his encouragement to Benjie and Harriet to make friends with clefs and crotchets. Sometimes she was called to help Harriet's piano practice, and stand with the twins singing scales, their first venture into songs.

The *signor*'s enthusiasm inspired them all. There followed a similar session in the afternoon, and a daily walk accompanied by Beth. Evenings were spent in musical indulgence, with the *signor* playing and singing requested pieces time and time again with unfailing geniality. Occasionally, Sophie read aloud for their pleasure, when the *signor*'s choices from the library were selected.

During the day, she seldom thought of Lord Adversane; but in the moments before sleep, he came to her mind. She tossed and turned. Grotesque thoughts as to his plight, revealed by Toby, emerged from the shadows. Though she longed to see him, she dreaded his return. How cruel that her days were filled with such enjoyments, yet he, the source of all her comfort, was threatened by the misery of ruination.

She rose readily enough these mornings for she found solitude worse than society, although she wished for the former more than the latter. Obliged to repress herself, she was less liable to the gloomy moods that swooped when she was unoccupied. Thus she was ready when Harriet came calling.

'Do you know what is happening today, Sophie?'

'Something special, judging by your bright little eyes.'

'Very special,' said Harriet, dogging Sophie as she dodged between the wardrobe and the dressing-table. 'You know that Benjie doesn't like playing the piano. Well, Basilio . . .'

'Basilio?'

'He wishes us to call him that instead of *signor*.'

'Ah, do go on . . .'

'Basilio has thought of a way to make Benjie play another instrument.'

'How has he achieved that?'

'With the help of Mr Haydn.'

'Mr Haydn?'

'Yes, come down now and Basilio will tell you himself.'

150

Holding hands with Harriet, who skipped all the way to the music salon, Sophie greeted the *signor* who was sorting music sheets.

'How is Mr Haydn helping you to interest Benjie in another instrument, pray?' she asked.

The *signor* smiled. 'Benjie will join us as soon as he has found what he is looking for.'

'*Signor!* Why so mysterious?'

'Please use my name—Basilio—as do my other pupils, Sophia.'

'I will do so. But, please elucidate upon Mr Haydn.'

His smile broadened. 'I was telling the twins of the background to the *Toy Symphony.* When Haydn was working near Vienna, he thought to buy a basketful of whistles, little fiddles, cuckoos and other instruments. Benjie told me he had a whistle which his Uncle Guy had bought for him at a country fair. I suggested he should bring it to this morning's session, and he is now looking for the whistle.'

'Oh, I hope he finds it,' said Sophie.

'I've arranged a little tune for him to start with. Who knows, we may have a future flautist in our midst.'

A shout of triumph preceded Benjie as he rushed into the salon, waving aloft the whistle. He joined them, placed his lips to the mouthpiece and produced a cacophony of sounds, forcing them to cover their ears.

'Now, Benjie,' said Basilio at last, 'you have

there a simple tin whistle with six holes. Let us put some order in those notes.'

Sophie left them at that point, seeking to join Beth for coffee. When later they both visited the salon, Benjie was playing his whistle to music which had been set for him on an adjusted stand. During the performance, Basilio joined in with the occasional chord on the piano which added ornament to Benjie's piece. He was flushed with pride when all applauded at the finish.

'Please let me play this again, Basilio.'

'You will certainly play it again, and also another piece which I shall arrange for you to play at our concert.'

Benjie eagerly nodded agreement.

That afternoon, though bright, the sun was veiled, the air humid and oppressive. Leaves were stilled and flowers motionless as if painted on a canvas.

Sophie, Beth, Basilio and the twins gathered on the terrace to take their usual walk, but shared a listlessness and reluctance to venture far.

'Perhaps we should stroll to the woods,' suggested Beth, 'where it may be cooler among the tall trees.'

They all agreed. Sophie and Beth loosely tied their bonnets, opened their fans and employed them immediately. Hatless, Basilio and the twins pressed ahead to escape the glare of the meadows for the deep shade of the woods.

In single file they explored the pathways. Apart from finding a rare orchid with white flowers, they came across a tangle of deadly nightshade. Dire warnings were passed to the twins to avoid it at all costs, especially in its berrying stage.

'A specific name for this plant is "Belladonna",' Basilio remarked, 'said to be used by Italian ladies for increasing the witchery of their eyes.'

'How so?' asked Sophie.

'It has the power of dilating the pupils.' With a laugh, he added: 'It may have done deadly work on unsuspecting men.'

'Have you been a victim, Basilio?' asked Beth, smiling.

A flush mounted his cheeks. 'I think I may have,' he said softly. 'A pair of dark eyes, bathed in transparent light—an indefinable perfection to make one gasp, *affascinante*, fascinating—this, my Rosa.'

There was a respectful silence from Beth and Sophie on hearing this artless disclosure, until Beth asked:

'Is Rosa in London, Basilio?'

He shook his head. 'She lives in Rome,' he replied in a manner which did not invite further enquiry.

They dawdled to a gap where the trees thinned. Breaking through to fields, they were shocked by the glowering skies.

'We'd better hasten. I think a storm threatens,' said Beth, taking the hands of the twins and running towards home. Sophie and Basilio followed at a slower pace, when a crash of thunder brought a sudden rainstorm with drops that pelted them like ha'pennies.

'Oh,' said Sophie, holding on to her bonnet. 'Look, there's a hedger's hut where we could shelter. The storm will soon pass.'

They ran across to the shed and stood within, stamping their feet and shaking off the raindrops. Basilio stood by the doorway watching the rain falling relentlessly.

Sophie removed her bonnet. She shook off the droplets lingering in the trimmings, joined the ribbon ties and placed them over her arm.

Basilio regarded her with amusement.

'The rain has played tricks with your bonnet.'

'Not so. Nell will reblock and retrim it as good as new,' she said, smoothing her hair. 'Basilio, I admire the way you persuaded Benjie to persevere with the tin whistle. His enthusiasm is touching.'

Basilio smiled. 'He doesn't like the piano but is prepared to tolerate it in duet mode with me.'

'He enjoys that.'

There was a silence, the only sound pelting of the rain. The hut was empty, except for a pile of sacks in a corner, and creepers invading the slatted walls infused a fragrance within.

Suddenly, Basilio spoke.

'Sophia, the lines of the song you wrote echo in my mind. I have composed a tune to suit them and insist it be included in our concert.'

She shook her head. 'It is not worthy of your time.'

'Allow that to be my decision.'

'I think the storm is on the wane,' she said, stepping to the doorway.

'But the rain is not, Sophia. Why did you call your song "Love's Measure" when you cannot measure love?'

'Love is a mystery, and I have simply made an attempt.' She looked away and toyed with an intrusive creeper.

There was a short, tense silence.

'Who inspired those words?' he asked softly. 'Is there someone as special to you as Rosa is to me?'

She blushed and bowed her head, murmuring, 'I don't know—but perhaps . . .'

'There *is* someone, then. Do not be afraid to admit it. I have noticed a wistfulness about you at times . . .'

'I see him so seldom.'

'Ah, that is my fate, too. I sometimes wonder whether I shall ever clasp my ideal to my heart.'

'He features in a dream I have.'

'Then you must chase that dream, Sophia,

insegua questo sogno!'

She closed her eyes, envisaging Guy's tender embrace at the fishing picnic, and his face so close to hers in the pony-phaeton. Chase that dream. She would, she vowed.

'We can go. The rain is almost stopped,' said Basilio, removing his coat and placing it around her shoulders.

'Thank you. It is wonderful to share secrets.'

'*Amicizia intensa*, the highest level of friendship.'

Dodging puddles and keeping to the short grass, they arrived at the house and entered through the kitchen, where they shed their muddy footwear before going to their rooms.

There was no sign of the twins, but Beth approached, flushed and breathless.

'Sophie, there is someone to see you! He awaits you in the salon anteroom.' Then, noting Sophie's shoeless state, she added: 'Put on some slippers and tidy your hair before you meet him.'

Beth turned promptly and left, affording no opportunity for further enlightenment.

'Perhaps it is he whom you see so seldom,' whispered Basilio, as he passed on his way to his apartment.

'Unlikely,' muttered Sophie, as she climbed the stairs to her room in a daze. Who could it be? Not the dreaded Anton, she hoped. Then she relaxed, smiling to herself. Of course, it must be Barty Wardyne, not yet called to the colours.

She replaced her hose, put on natural-kid slippers, grey sarcenet gown and the lilac-velvet spencer. Her hair had become unkempt in the rain, so she brushed it vigorously and tied it into a top-knot with a black ribbon, allowing curly tendrils to frame her face. Recalling the light-hearted Barty, she ran happily down the stairs and was broadly smiling a welcome as she entered the anteroom. A tall figure by the window turned towards her. It was Lord Adversane.

She gasped, meeting his gaze as her breath quickened. He stood regarding her, hands clasped behind his back. There fell a benign silence between them, with Sophie aware only of the mantel clock ticking away in unison with her heart.

Suddenly, he took a step towards her. A kindly expression enlivened his sea-grey eyes as he tilted his head.

'Sophie, whose daughter are you?' he asked.

She wanted to laugh aloud at this amazing question which had disrupted their shared silence, but she tempered it with a bright smile.

'As well you know, my lord, I am the daughter of Captain Sir John Stapleford . . .'

'You are incorrect, Sophie,' he interposed.

She frowned, and was about to respond, when he continued: 'You are the daughter of Sir John Stapleford who is no longer a captain but a rear-admiral of the Blue in His Majesty's

157

Navy. *The Times* reports that he is awarded this promotion, and I am informed it is likely the Prince Regent will make your father vice-admiral when he returns to these shores.'

Her eyes widened as she pressed her hands to her cheeks in a gesture of delight.

'Oh,' she breathed, and again, 'Oh!' Then, she lowered her head as tears brimmed in her eyes, murmuring, 'Thank you for this wonderful news, my lord.'

He approached and placed his hands gently upon her shoulders. She felt the sweet surprise of his touch.

'There's more,' he whispered, taking her hand and leading her to a settle. He sat beside her, smiling and retaining her hand. 'I am grateful to Jack Watts for this information. Seeing the joy in your response, Sophie, gives me pleasure since I've longed to give you hope about your father's fate.' He shook his head. 'You would marvel at the subterfuge employed in its conveyance—night-rides to remote villages and unheard-of taverns. Great care must be observed as Napoleon's spies are active. I came directly here, impelled by eagerness to impart this to you.'

All this time she had thought him to be in London; but now composed, she regarded him with such happiness as she had never known before, marking his strength of jaw, lips tilting in a smile, eyes eloquent with feeling. He had touched her heart, for she was sure he was speaking from his own.

'Oh, my lord,' she whispered, 'I cannot thank you enough. Words seem inadequate to express my gratitude to you and your friend.'

'Sophie, there is more to say. These accolades have increased your father's value to the French, but there's a disparity in bargaining for his release. The French insist that at least four French officers be freed in the exchange, and they may now demand even more. Though their requests have been refused, the matter is still extant and contacts are maintained. Think, Sophie, how wonderful it will be when agreement is reached!'

Her eyes shone, and Guy felt a quick pulse of delight at the rapture his news had wrought in her.

The door opened and Beth appeared, followed by a footman with a tray of glasses and decanters.

'I think it fitting we should celebrate. Do you not agree, Sophie?' Beth smiled.

Sophie leapt to greet her.

'Oh, you know!' she cried.

Beth nodded, as she embraced her.

'I'm so happy for you.'

Guy dismissed the footman and began to serve the wine. He had arrived at Rothervale drenched from the thunderstorm. Beth had taken his cloak to be dried in the kitchen and, seated together, he had told her that which he had related to Sophie. He had withheld from them Jack's warning, that in the event of the prisoner exchange failing, or the admiral escaping or being rescued, the vengeful French might attempt abduction of his daughter as a bargaining factor. He thought grimly that, in his role as her guardian, Sophie's safety must now be paramount among his concerns.

They talked of plans for the admiral's eventual return; but Guy was troubled by the fact that, upon a reply from Sir Henry, he would soon be obliged to leave for London on his own affairs.

He was suddenly aware that Beth was addressing him.

'You must stay tonight, Guy. I will give instructions for your room to be readied.'

He rose to his feet. 'I cannot remain a moment more, Beth. I have been absent from Adversane for the good part of a week, and I'm sure a letter from Sir Henry awaits me. So, I must leave immediately.' He raised them both to their feet and took their hands. 'Promise me that you will keep secret all I have said, convey it to no one.'

They nodded. He kissed their hands and took his leave.

He mounted Japhet, who had been well tended by the grooms after his wetting, and began his way to Adversane. It had been a day of high winds and torrential rain, and afternoon was closing in with shadows.

He thought of Sophie, tear-blinded, as he

held her. Some inner indefinable feeling had caught him unawares. He had to admit she was indeed beautiful, elegant, unaffected in her manner and unaware of her power of enchantment; gentlemen's glances would hover and pause. Now there was this threat of Napoleon's reach into their pastoral paradise which demanded enhanced protection of a serious kind on her guardian's part. He set his lips and increased pace.

The rosy fingers of a setting sun pinked the grey sky like the slashed sleeves of a doublet as he approached the environs of the park. Suddenly, he reined in. Sophie had so captivated him that he omitted to ask Beth whether Anton's visit was imminent. He would have dismissed it from his mind had Jack not placed a strange emphasis on his French *émigré* friend. Jack had cautioned that there were those in London who wore the Bourbon cockade on their hats but not in their hearts. Should Anton agree to carry out certain tasks for the Napoleonists, they would ensure that he repossessed his Poitiers estates as a reward. His proximity to Sophie might signify extreme danger. Guy snapped into a canter and, cursing himself, determined to send a note to Beth to ascertain the position.

As he came up the darkened drive, grooms gathered to take Japhet to his stable. Wearily, Guy entered the house. Lewis met him in the hall.

161

'My lord, Sir Henry Nancarrow arrived early this morning. He is settled in the best apartment and, presumably, will sup with you this evening if that is agreeable, my lord.'

'Of course, Lewis. Do whatever is necessary to make him comfortable.'

Guy frowned. Sir Henry here? Were Adversane affairs so disastrous that he felt it imperative to convey bad news in person? On the other hand, his arrival could be a boon, especially if it precluded Guy from a visit to London. Should Anton call at Rothervale, Guy would be ready to go to Sophie's aid without delay.

CHAPTER TEN

As Guy changed for an evening repast with Sir Henry, his valet Lewis said:

'While you were away, my lord, Seb Broadrib came to the house to tell you that Hynde Hallam has left Adversane and taken up lodgings at the Tabard.'

Guy frowned. 'The Tabard?'

'A tavern of ill-repute near Five Oaks, my lord.'

'Not too far from here. In the absence of a formal response to my letter, I presume it to be a permanent removal on his part. Please tell Seb I will see him so soon as I have spoken with Sir Henry.'

Lewis nodded as he withdrew.

Guy had displayed Mrs Lachbone's paintings on a long mahogany table in the octagon room, where the window-blinds had been drawn and the door locked as a precaution, despite Hallam's reported departure. Guy would retreat there with Sir Henry for dessert to conclude their evening meal.

Before leaving to join Sir Henry, he penned a note to Beth asking her to inform him immediately Anton arrived at Rothervale. Satisfied that he was taking a first step in his mission to protect Sophie, he left eagerly to meet Sir Henry for an *aperitif* in the salon anteroom. He was already seated there, and rose to shake hands warmly.

'Welcome to Adversane, Sir Henry,' said Guy. 'I trust you are well rested. Lewis tells me he prepared the apartment you have used on previous visits, and I hope it's suitable for your present needs.'

'It's excellent, and I'm grateful to Lewis for accommodating my valet and Mr Bodmin, our chief clerk.'

Guy turned and signalled to a footman.

'I trust you will enjoy a fine sherry with me before we dine,' he said.

Sir Henry nodded approvingly as he returned to his chair.

'Which reminds me,' continued Guy, 'that

163

our revered Sir John Stapleford, languishing in France, has been raised to rear-admiral.'

'I hope there are plans afoot for a prisoner exchange.'

'I am assured that is proceeding.'

'And what of Miss Stapleford? Is she aware of this?'

'Miss Stapleford is presently bestowed with my sister at Rothervale, and was overjoyed when she was told.'

There was a silence as the footman served the sherry. They raised their glasses to the new rear-admiral and drank a toast to each other. A short pause followed.

'I've heard it said that there is nothing makes a man suspect much, more than to know little,' Guy then remarked. 'I am smitten with curiosity. Am I right in thinking that matters are somewhat calamitous, hence your journey to Adversane?'

Sir Henry pursed his lips. 'Not entirely calamitous. There is a way forward.'

'You should know that Hallam has left the estate and is lodged in a tavern a short way from here.'

'That does not surprise me. It is obvious he has been instructed not to leave the vicinity.'

Guy frowned at this and drew breath. He quickly drained his glass and stood to help Sir Henry from his chair, prior to leading him into the dining-salon.

'We shan't risk spoiling an excellent repast

with disclosures about Hallam. Come, all is ready.'

Candlelight glowed on white floor-length tablecloths, and the cutlery, porcelain and plate gleamed. As they dined, the purpose of their meeting was avoided in their converse. Instead, Guy enthused over the steeplechase course, in which fervour Sir Henry joined with great interest.

'It may surprise you, Guy, but your venture is raising excitement at Tattersall's and the clubs. The first Saturday in October is firmly on the calendar.'

Guy was pleased to hear this, but was puzzled by Sir Henry's remark that Hallam *had been instructed not to leave the vicinity.* Who was manipulating the Hallam puppet-strings?

Later, after dessert in the octagon room, Guy placed additional candelabra on the mahogany table fully to reveal Mrs Lachbone's paintings.

'Do you recall, Sir Henry,' said Guy, 'at our first meeting to discuss the inheritance, you warned me that something irregular was going on at Adversane. These paintings will give you some idea of the extent of those irregularities. The forests and meadows pictured here are now a wasteland; timber has been taken out and there has been systematic removal of gravel. This hamlet,' he continued, indicating the Nether Cherry paintings, 'has been

165

demolished.'

Sir Henry moved slowly around the table, bending over the pictures and closely examining them. After some moments, he straightened and returned to his chair. He sat in silence, head bowed and hands clasped in his lap. Then he looked up.

'The total of your claim, Guy, is presumably for material taken out, combined with an estimate for reparation.'

'Indeed, yes. Fifteen thousand guineas.'

'The counterclaim is for the exact amount of your claim, made up by forged promissory notes to your father's account.'

'Who is the claimant?'

'It is time for Mr Bodmin to join us, Guy.'

'Of course. He must share a wine-posset with us,' said Guy, already at the bell-pull. He returned to his chair. 'I shall employ the paintings as a guide to the restoration. The poor souls who were evicted from Nether Cherry are constantly in my mind, and the first task will be to build a new hamlet there,' said Guy.

'The paintings should serve you well for that purpose.'

The door opened and a footman appeared. Guy gave instructions for Mr Bodmin to attend immediately and ordered the drinks. He placed a chair alongside Sir Henry for the taciturn Mr Bodmin, who lost no time in joining them. He bowed to Guy before taking

166

his seat.

'His lordship has asked me a direct question, Mr Bodmin, and I require your help in answering it,' said Sir Henry.

Mr Bodmin nodded as Guy posed his question once more.

'The claimant is an associate of Mr Hallam, my lord, by name of The Skull in London,' answered Mr Bodmin.

'The Skull in London!' repeated Guy, incredulously.

'I'm afraid so,' interposed Sir Henry. 'It is an awesome link to the underworld operating in the stews of the Seven Dials. Mr Gabe Driscoll, using the last syllable of his surname as a nickname for sinister intent, is much feared, an incessant gambler and active in every kind of criminality.'

'And Hallam is an associate of this man!'

Mr Bodmin continued. 'Working in the law, it is incumbent upon me to be acquainted with the criminal world and its workings. Several informants aid me in such investigations. Hallam passes funds from the plunder directly to The Skull and they planned for further exploitation. The Skull is angered that all has ceased upon your lordship's return to Adversane. He covets the entire estate.'

At this Guy's fist crashed upon the table.

'The King's Bench!' he thundered. Then, endeavouring to control his outrage, turned to Sir Henry. 'This must be brought before the

King's Bench! There's no time to be lost!'

Sir Henry shook his head sadly. 'I know Adversane is vulnerable, but haste is not the issue here. The Skull is adept at dodging all attempts to bring him to justice. Your claim will fail if pursued within the jurisdiction of the Court of the King's Bench.'

'How can this be?' demanded Guy.

Sir Henry motioned to Mr Bodmin.

'My lord,' replied the chief clerk, 'servers of writs are denied the opportunity to carry out their duties. The Skull is forewarned of their approach and vanishes to hiding-places that are legion and ever-changing. He is slippery as a fish. There are numerous writs against him, but some Runners are in his pay and take no remedial action.'

A footman entered bearing the posset-cup and glasses on a tray. As they were served, Guy left his chair and returned to ponder the paintings again. Suddenly and overwhelmingly, Adversane became very dear to him. He thought of his father, of Nether Cherry and his loyal retainers, his valued tenants, the Admiral and Sophie. Ah, Sophie . . .

A touch upon his shoulder made him turn abruptly. He stared angrily at the benign countenance of Sir Henry.

'Guy, there is an alternative to a lawsuit,' he said softly. 'I will dismiss Bodmin after we have partaken of our refreshment, so that we may discuss a plan which might promise

168

success.'

Guy sighed heavily, returned to his seat and privately raised his glass to a successful conclusion. Pleasantries were exchanged as to the rural splendour of Adversane until Mr Bodmin, taking his cue from Sir Henry, politely withdrew.

Guy drained his glass at one gulp.

'What must I do?' he asked briskly.

'You have told me of the new steeplechase course you have set out at Adversane, due to open in October. You must make sure it catches the interest of all Tattersall's patrons, gentry and commoners alike. Invite "Equinus", Mr Pearley, to Adversane to inspect the course and extol it in his writings. Set all those tulips of the turf buzzing with excitement about this new venue for a race and a gamble.'

'This sounds like a diversion, Sir Henry.'

'On the contrary, Guy. I am relying on the new steeplechase course becoming a popular topic, bound to come to the ears of The Skull. Its location at Adversane will act as a bait. He lives by gambling for high stakes.'

There was a silence.

'Please proceed,' said Guy.

'I am seeking to change the claims into Debts of Honour.'

'Surely a misnomer, should it concern The Skull,' said Guy with a wry smile.

'Such debts are contracted by betting or gambling, so called because they are not legally recoverable. An old saying declares there's honour among thieves. In this wise, The Skull dare not leave any gambling debt unpaid. It would sully his reputation.'

'Would he accept this?'

'With alacrity, it avoids a court of law. The Skull's claim on you is for so-called promissory notes for sums advanced to your father—all fraudulently produced by his army of calligraphers. If we seek to establish the claim and counterclaim as Debts of Honour—as if gambling debts—this would give credence to his forgeries, something he cannot ignore.' Sir Henry leaned forward, engaging Guy without levity. 'Are you confident you could win that closing race?'

'Supremely so,' said Guy, brightening. 'Jem and Brisket could do it with ease!'

Sir Henry nodded. 'I shall draw up the wager in the correct terms, present it to The Skull, and lodge it at Tattersall's in the accepted form, inviting the entry of his own horse and rider to meet your challenge. You would have to permit his minions reasonable access to the course in due time. With a high stake, he would find it irresistible.'

'And that stake is the amount of our claim,' said Guy.

Sir Henry rose. 'The stake is the equivalent of Adversane itself!'

Mists had gathered on the riverbank bridle-path, which persuaded Sophie to take her morning ride in the brightening higher fields.

Correctly habited, she sought a quiet, meandering ride to savour the fleeting visit of Lord Adversane. He had imparted the wonderful news of her father in a way that left her elated and full of hope in every sense. Her delight knew no bounds in reliving that moment of shared rapture, when he had held her and regarded her with unstinted tenderness. In all his ways there was a conquering charm, such natural grace, and something sweet and proud.

Afterwards, she had talked with Beth, who told her that she had seldom seen her brother so happy since his return to Adversane.

'It is in your power, Sophie,' she had added mysteriously.

Jet gave a prodigious bound, expecting to gallop, but she curbed him.

'Not this morning, Jet,' she murmured, recalling those rides of sheer abandon with Gorran, the gypsy. She wondered where he was and if she would ever see him again.

Slowly, she guided Jet down the hill to the river. The sun, now risen, bestowed a transparency to the air, not a vestige of mist remained. She watched the river wend its gleaming way. For the last mile, she put Jet to

171

a canter and, near home, welcomed Gus and Gussie to pace beside her.

After stabling Jet, she walked to the kitchen, passing the carriage house on the way. There she saw grooms attending two bay horses, unhitched from a carriage she did not recognize. Neighbours calling, she thought, deciding in that case to take breakfast in her room.

She changed into a grey cambric morning-dress and hastened to the music salon, where she knew Basilio was awaiting her. The music concert was only two weeks away, and Basilio insisted on practising her song daily, at every opportunity. She dreaded it, despite his praise, and tried not to be tardy for the rehearsals.

Sounds of Harriet's piano solo reached Sophie as she left her room. It pleased her that the twins' enthusiasm had not flagged, and Basilio's delight was evident. As she entered, she heard Basilio persuading Harriet to play the piece again '. . . so that Sophia might hear it.' Without hesitation, Harriet did so, her fingers floating over the keys with consummate ease, and Basilio turning the music page for her.

Sophie applauded and hugged Harriet, who shrugged and smiled.

'There are some very grand people coming to the concert,' she said. 'I hope I'll not disappoint.' Sophie joined with Basilio in expressions of encouragement.

'Now it is Sophia's turn,' said Basilio, seating himself at the piano. 'I think it might be a good idea to repeat the last line of each quatrain as a reprise. Simply sing it twice. Let us rehearse the last verse with that in mind.'

Sophie stood in the curve of the piano, facing Basilio as he played the introduction. He had composed a romantic air, set in a key to suit her mezzo-soprano voice and fitting her words to perfection. He lifted his hand for her to begin. With a deep breath, she began to sing the last verse:

> *'Your kingdom knows no measure,*
> *Dimensions have no part.*
> *With you is boundless pleasure,*
> *Supreme of all my heart,*
> *Supreme of all my heart.'*

Basilio beamed, and Harriet clasped Sophie's hand.

'That was magical, Sophie,' she whispered.

To Sophie's surprise, others in the music salon came forward, applauding. She had not realized she was singing to company. Beth approached with a gentleman in dandyish finery who was smiling sardonically. Sophie recognized the darkly handsome looks of Monseigneur Anton-Alexandre, Comte de Saint-Gabriel.

She froze in surprise as Beth effected the introductions between the *comte* and Basilio.

173

The *comte* made a motion as if to kiss Sophie's hand, but she quickly bobbed a curtsy in greeting.

'May we request an encore?' He smiled.

Basilio looked askance at Sophie, but she shook her head.

The *comte* bowed graciously.

'We shall all meet for a drink before the evening meal,' said Beth, withdrawing with the *comte*, followed by Harriet.

'*Dio mio!* You are troubled, Sophia. Is this French aristo he whom you see so seldom?'

'Certainly not!' she replied, with emphasis. 'I should prefer not to see him at all!'

Basilio shook his head sadly as he closed the piano.

'Are you happy with the repetition in your song, Sophia? Only if it meets your approval shall we do it.'

'Yes, I am happy with the new idea,' she answered, making preparations to leave.

Basilio caught her hand. 'I shall always be here to listen, Sophia—not only to your song . . .'

She smiled. 'I know, Basilio. Thank you.'

She walked quickly to the salon anteroom where she hoped to find Beth alone. She opened the door and peeped inside.

'Come in, Sophie,' said Beth. 'I am anxious to see you. Anton is now surveying the games gallery, where he will be working. Let us share a pot of coffee.'

Sophie entered with relief, tempered by the need to know how long Anton was likely to stay. She thought of her last encounter with the *comte* in her father's room, and of the letter he had sent to her which Guy claimed was full of untruths. Disturbed by the *comte*'s sudden appearance, tremors of excitement tinged with fear coursed through her.

'You have no idea how I have dreaded this predicament,' said Beth, handing a cup of coffee to Sophie.

'Predicament, Beth?'

'Yes. Two young and handsome continental gentlemen staying as our guests at the same time, places a great responsibility upon me as your chaperon, especially in the absence of Toby and Guy.'

Sophie blushed. 'I'm sure both Basilio and Anton will conduct themselves admirably,' she replied, confident insofar as Basilio was concerned and merely expressing a hope in the case of Anton.

'Guy intended to call upon Anton in London and request that he postpone his visit. He will be incensed at Anton's presence here.'

Sophie felt a stab of pleasure at Beth's words. She thought of Guy and wondered how matters were proceeding in his claim. When would he come again to Rothervale?

'. . . best to make sure you are not left alone with either gentleman, Sophie,' Beth was saying.

'That is not possible when Basilio and I rehearse my song for the concert.'

Beth nodded. 'That is excusable, I suppose. Perhaps Nell should attend you while these gentlemen are with us.'

'Oh, that is not necessary,' protested Sophie. 'I will conduct myself with all necessary decorum in their presence.'

Beth had received Guy's note, asking her to let him know immediately Anton arrived at Rothervale; but at the same time he had mentioned Sir Henry's arrival at Adversane. After this chat with Sophie, she decided not to inform him, convinced that, now forewarned, nothing would go amiss.

Sophie was soon reassured. Anton's behaviour was without fault and no longer a source of annoyance. He was actively engaged on clearing a disused building near the stables and there establishing three fencing-pistes. When their paths crossed, Sophie was set at ease by his polite formality.

The idyllic routine of music in the mornings and accompanied walks in the afternoon was maintained. Anton joined them for meals and in the evenings for entertainment provided by Basilio. Since there was now a foursome, Beth arranged for the occasional game of cards.

After a long night of music and cards, Sophie joined Beth in the salon anteroom to sip some wine before retiring. Beth told her she had sent invitations to friends and neighbours for the music concert, and consulted with staff outlining the preparations. She was happy that it was high summer and garden flowers and fruits were abundant.

Beth rose. 'Come, Sophie, it's very late. The gentlemen were abed long ago.' She embraced and kissed her, smilingly cupping her face and murmuring: 'Goodnight, my dear. Your being so fair adds to my difficulties.'

Sophie took up a lighted taper from the hall table, and bade Beth sleep well. As she mounted the stairs to her room, the taper guttered. Sheilding it with her hand, she paused to look from the landing window, and gasped at the splendour of the moonlit garden dappled in shadows. For some moments, she stood entranced, then suddenly realized she was not alone. Silently regarding her from the curtain at the side of the window was the Comte de Saint-Gabriel, clad in a black military-style robe.

She gasped, and stepped back.

'My lord . . .'

'Do not be alarmed,' he whispered. 'I, too, enjoy the moon-light.' He slipped a smile, snuffed the flame of the taper before taking it from her and placed it on the wide ledge.

She turned to continue to her room, but he caught her hand.

'My lord!' she said, with admonishment in her voice.

'It has been impossible to speak to you

alone, so I sought to waylay you. Where is your most honourable guardian? I thought it likely he would be here.'

Her hand remained firmly in his grasp.

'By now he should be in London,' she answered, her heart beating fast.

'Ah,' smiled the *comte*. 'The lovely Charlotte will be happy now that you have released him to her.'

His words stung her like a lash. She tried vainly to recall Guy's denials, but they paled beside the *comte*'s confident assertion. She endeavoured to regain her composure.

'He is there to settle matters concerned with his estate and . . .'

'And,' he interposed, 'to determine the whereabouts of your father?'

There was a strange edge to his voice as he posed this question, and it gave her pause. Guy had forbidden discussion with others on matters concerning her father. She respected that and would observe it.

'You were saying?' he pressed.

'. . . and he will call here on his way back to Adversane. We expect him very soon.'

There was an uneasy silence as clouds darkened the moon. In the half-light, his eyes glowed as he gazed at her. '*Mon Dieu*, you are exquisite, my dear Miss Stapleford.'

She gave no answer and, frowning, tried to free her hand, but he did not relent.

'The words of your song are appropriate;

for in truth, I could endow you with boundless pleasure. Tell me, would you grant me the honour of considering me your suitor? I have estates in France—a position at Court . . .'

'My lord, kindly release my hand so that I may continue to my room.'

'I have asked you a question, and shall await your answer,' he whispered. He raised her hand to his lips and progressed lingeringly with kisses along the length of her arm. She flinched and jerked away from him.

Smiling, he said: '*A bientôt, mon amour!*'

Abruptly, she turned and walked grandly to her room. For the first time she felt it necessary to lock the door. She undressed and, in the comforting darkness, trembled with rancour at the *comte*'s insolence. She briskly ran her hand down her arm several times as if to brush away those kisses, then surrendered to sleep while yearning for the bliss of such intimacy with Guy.

CHAPTER ELEVEN

Apart from seeking to engage Sophie's eyes at every opportunity, Anton reverted to the polite formality he had practised before their moonlight encounter. Their meetings were occasional and brief; she spent most of the day rehearsing with Basilio and the twins, and with

Beth to aid in preparations for the concert.

Taking a rest from their duties, Sophie sat with Beth on the terrace in the bright morning sun, shaded by parasols.

'Basilio and his musician friends will be costumed in eighteenth-century mode for the event,' mused Beth. 'While I shall follow that theme for the twins, I think you should present yourself in a gown of the very latest fashion and in a colour a tiny step out of mourning. What do you think, Sophie?'

Sophie drew breath. 'Oh—is that necessary, a new gown?'

Beth smiled. 'I think so. It has been on my mind for some weeks, and my mantua-maker visits us this afternoon. You shall meet her.'

'I hadn't thought of that aspect of the concert.'

'The Wardynes have accepted. Barty may be present as he's not yet been called abroad and is still in London. Toby will be bringing a small party and other neighbours have responded, too. It will be a goodly company, and I know Guy intends to come,' said Beth.

'But is he not in London?'

'No. I received a note that Sir Henry Nancarrow is visiting him at Adversane.'

Happy that Guy was nearby, Sophie hoped that Sir Henry's visit would resolve the estate affairs.

'Benjie refuses to wear a wig for his performance,' Beth continued, 'but he agrees to a velvet coat and breeches similar to Basilio's. Harriet is delighted to wear a simple panniered gown and have her hair powdered.'

'They'll make a charming little couple,' murmured Sophie, still thinking of Guy.

At the song-rehearsal with Basilio that day, Sophie suddenly felt confident that it would perform well. Basilio instructed on timing, expression, posture, and appeared delighted in her attempts.

'Sing your song to everyone, Sophia,' he urged. 'Embrace the audience with your eyes. All must learn "Love's Measure"—the words are so beautiful.'

'More so in your musical treatment of them, Basilio.'

'An example of our shared talents.'

She smiled. 'For the first time, I am looking forward to the concert.'

'As am I, *cara mia*,' he said softly, closing the piano.

She nodded approvingly, then ran lightly up the stairs to keep an appointment with Beth and the mantua-maker.

Mounds of shining taffeta in every shade of blue graced Madame Corinne's work table. Beth draped a length over Sophie's shoulder. 'This, I think, Madame?'

'*Mais oui!* A beautiful shade for her! A low flounce in matching gauze?' suggested Madame, seizing a sample, 'attached with brilliants.'

'Wonderful!' Beth exclaimed, smiling at Sophie. 'Come to the mirror and see.'

Sophie did so. 'Oh, Beth!' she gasped. 'How lovely!'

Beth then selected the material for her own gown. A rich russet-and-black striped silk simply styled with a matching head-dress. Sophie hugged her. 'You will look full of magical charm, Beth.'

'So will you, Sophie—magical and musical!'

Sophie then submitted to being measured for her new gown, and Madame arranged to return the next day for first fittings.

Sophie was overwhelmed by Basilio's praise of her song's performance. This, combined with Madame's flattery when trying on her new gown, added to her joy. She felt the concert to be a turning-point in persuading Guy that she had been worthy of his beneficence. Her excitement grew as she wished the days away.

After her own fitting, she remained to see Beth step into her new gown. It took shape, rustling as Madame pinned and tacked the shimmering silk. A tap on the door caused all to turn.

'Who is it?' called Beth.

'It's Esther, my lady.'

'The nursery nurse. Come in, Esther.'

'Sorry, my lady, I thought the twins might be with you. They are late for their tea.'

'They are probably with Anton in the games

room. He is teaching Benjie to fence,' said Beth. 'I'm unable to come at the moment, Esther, but . . .'

'I'll go with Esther to the games room and take the twins back to the nursery,' said Sophie, rising.

'Thank you, Sophie. Make sure you come back together.'

'Of course,' said Sophie. She left with Esther.

They walked across the lawns towards the stable block. A small building adjacent to the stables had once housed hunting-trophies, and it was here that Anton had measured out three fencing pistes. The room was panelled, with a high wooden ceiling; its emptiness made it a place of echoes.

They found Anton stripped of his coat, in a fine cambric shirt, instructing Benjie in simple sword-play, watched by Harriet. As Sophie entered she heard Anton proclaiming a taunting: '*Avancez, avancez!*' to Benjie, while parrying his thrusts to devastating effect.

'Come, your tea is ready!' called Sophie.

Harriet came to her side immediately, but Benjie turned and playfully brandished his foil at her. Feigning terror, she placed her hands over her face while Benjie danced a jig around her. Then she suddenly chased the twins away with Esther. She was about to follow, when she was startled by the metallic clatter of Anton's foil coming to rest at her feet.

'A duel, Miss Stapleford?' asked Anton, mockingly.

She looked down at the handle and pommel expertly positioned for a response to the challenge.

'Am I called out, then?' she replied, curtly.

'You should be called out, for you have wounded me as sure as any blade.'

She turned to go, but Anton stepped in front of her and stood with his back to the door, preventing her departure.

'My lord,' she demanded, 'please allow me to pass.'

'I cannot let you pass until you answer the question I posed. Agree that I may court you, and I will ask your guardian's blessing.'

She shook her head. 'I cannot consent to anything more than friendship.'

He turned and spat out a word which she took to be an oath. Her heart beat wildly with sudden fear of him. With one stride, he gathered her into his arms and crushed her lips in a kiss so fervent that it was deeply mortifying. She struggled, but his grip tightened.

'Grant my request, then I can abandon desperate acts and thoughts to that purpose,' he whispered, his eyes coursing her face.

She mustered her strength and pushed him away.

'If friendship is not sufficient then I must withdraw my company from you, and so inform my guardian.'

He regarded her sullenly as she stepped back from him. 'My proposal is bound to be favoured by your guardian,' he said. 'Ask yourself, who is it he courts at Dynes Park?'

Her cheeks burned. 'What do you mean?' she sputtered. She watched him strut in front of her, not failing to mark the impact of these words upon her. His blade had struck.

'Why are you here at Rothervale? To refine you for the London Season, the marriage market. The earl wants you off his hands and he's willing for you to go to the first contender provided he measures up to your social position. A French *comte* is the equivalent of an English earl, is he not? Should you tell him of my offer, he would accept it without demur.'

Sophie turned her back on him. She covered her ears to hear no more.

'My father would not permit that I marry against my will, nor would the earl who acts in his stead!' she cried.

He smiled. 'The earl has many things on his mind. If his claim goes to court, it will finish him. On the long list of affairs that affect him, he would not care one iota whether you are willing or not. To relinquish his guardianship is one matter less to deal with.'

'I do not believe you!'

He picked up the fencing foil. 'Remember, he is *mon ami*,' he said, quietly. 'I know of these things.'

She fled from him. She reached her room and sat by the window, weeping quietly. Chagrin soon replaced despair as she realized her reactions had revealed too much. In their duel of words and feelings, Anton had been the victor.

In preparing for the evening meal, she decided to behave as though nothing had happened to upset her. She felt better for her resolve to show Anton that what had passed between them was of no consequence.

At the rehearsal the next day, Sophie found difficulty in maintaining her enthusiasm. Her spirits plummeted as Anton's words possessed her mind. *Ask yourself, who is it he courts at Dynes Park?* There was no need to speculate. Had she not witnessed Lady Charlotte's intimate approach to her guardian? Yet his response by no means confirmed interest; but doubts abounded because of Anton's taunt.

In the middle of the last quatrain of her song, Basilio suddenly stopped playing. 'It is hopeless, Sophia. What has happened, where are your thoughts?'

She bowed her head. 'I am sorry, Basilio. Tomorrow will be better.'

'This has never happened since we have worked together. What has occurred to so change your mood?' She was unable to reply lest he see her eyes brimming. 'Tell me, Sophia.'

She swallowed and faced him. 'The *comte*

186

has raised doubts about my guardian.'

'Ah, he whom you see so seldom and is the core of your dream?'

She nodded. Basilio shrugged. 'Perhaps the *comte* has a dream of his own.'

'You are perceptive, Basilio.'

He pursed his lips. 'Keep to your own dream, Sophia. Do not allow the *comte* or anyone to deprive you of it.'

She pondered, then sighed deeply. 'I shall try to do so.'

He took her hand and lightly kissed it. 'I cannot stand by and watch you brought down without attempting to raise you to your usual height of joyous singing. You are beautiful and young. Though I have never met him, I hear your guardian is an honourable gentleman. He'll not disappoint you.'

'Dear Basilio, you make me full of hope,' she said.

'Let us rehearse tomorrow, Sophia, when I shall expect perfection,' he replied with a smile.

A transformation was taking place in the house and grounds. Beth, aided by Basilio, directed the joiners as to the placement and height of the dais in the main salon. In every window embrasure, bronzed-iron flower-stands appeared, each with brackets to hold cut flowers of every hue and variety.

Sophie welcomed the diversion of carrying out the tasks assigned to her, one of which was to select blooms for the window stands, assisted by Mr Tilt, the head gardener.

This morning, Beth joined them. She handed Sophie a trug, gloves and cutting-knife and drew her aside.

'I have received a message from Lady Wardyne, Sophie. She is expecting Guy to call at Dynes Park to escort someone from there to the concert. Do you suppose it is Lady Charlotte?'

Sophie could hardly respond. She felt drained at this, and simply shrugged.

'If Lady Charlotte is still a guest there, then it must be she,' she mumbled.

'I wonder,' said Beth.

Mr Tilt awaited them by the conservatory. He bowed in greeting, and turned to lead the way to the rose-garden.

Sophie, still affected by Beth's revelation, was none the less charmed by the varied fragrance of the roses.

Mr Tilt indicated which of the barely opened buds they should pick.

'These,' he said grandly, 'are the China roses, but we shall proceed to the French roses, which are excellent just now.'

To Sophie, there were no distinctions; all were perfect in their own way. She wandered ahead, and stooped to examine a purplish rose at the end of a broken stem.

'May we not pick this one? It is in full bloom but its stem is damaged.'

Mr Tilt rushed forward.

'Be careful with that one, Miss Sophie. We admire its blossoms but approach it with caution.'

'Why so?' asked Sophie.

'It is a *Rosa bourboniana* named the "Anton-Alexandre".'

'Oh,' said Sophie, with awakening interest. 'What are its shortcomings?'

'It is handsome but its thorns are numerous and sharp like the claw of a bird. They draw blood at the least touch.'

She had no difficulty in believing this. She watched with pleasure as Mr Tilt severed the bloom and, at the same time, clipped off its awesome thorns.

Adversane

Guy bade farewell to Sir Henry who, to his regret, could not remain for the concert at Rothervale. He and Mr Bodmin were anxious to deal with the steeplechase wager, and would send Guy a progress report by courier from London.

Guy watched their coach pass through the gates, then turned and walked slowly to the stables, deep in thought. A debt of honour was not recognized by law but was binding in honour, especially when it applied to gambling and betting debts. Would The Skull be persuaded to regard the claim and counterclaim as gambling debts collectable on the outcome of a steeplechase? Sir Henry and Mr Bodmin assured him The Skull would agree to this, knowing his partiality for high-stakes gambling. If so, and Brisket won, Adversane would be safe, and the funds forthcoming would be applied to the rebuilding of Nether Cherry and the reclamation of the forests. If not, he would be forced to sell Adversane. It was a formidable gamble.

He arrived at the stables to see Jem bringing out the mighty Brisket. The gelding's noble frame and extreme energy guaranteed him a match for any horse The Skull might enter. Guy stroked him and rested his forehead against the grey's warm flank. 'It's all up to you, Brisket,' he muttered.

With Seb he watched Jem mount and trot away to the course.

'I'll join the runs whenever I can,' Guy said to Seb.

He returned to the house to prepare for the early evening visit to Rothervale for the concert. He welcomed the diversion and was eager to see Sophie, having thought of her often. He hoped to please her by a gift of flowers for the occasion, and had selected a spray of cultivated violets, similar to those she had worn on her dress for their drive in the pony-phaeton, which he had not forgotten. He had sent a footman to deliver them to Rothervale.

Happily musing on her reaction, he suddenly hastened. It had almost slipped his mind that he must first call at Dynes Park.

CHAPTER TWELVE

Guy's flowers had taken her breath away. As Nell helped Sophie into the new gown, she could see how beautifully it toned with the deep purple-and-white array of the violets. They would soften the daringly low neckline that Madame had insisted upon. Nell dressed her hair into the curled top style she favoured, and a blue band extended to a full bow at the back.

'You are beautiful, Miss Sophie,' said Nell as she stepped back to admire her. 'Your eyes are bluer than ever!'

Sophie smiled, acknowledging the compliment. She should feel happy and confident, but curiosity persisted as to the identity of the person Guy was escorting from Dynes Park.

Toby had arrived last evening with guests. Later that morning, Sophie had shared a light luncheon with both Toby and Beth who persuaded her to return to her room for a rest before dressing. She had done so; but, now ready, she crept downstairs to see the decorated salon.

Flowers filled every window embrasure and candelabra stood ready for the first hint of dusk. The dais, carpeted green, was occupied by Basilio's friends preparing their instruments and sheet music, while the piano was adorned with a large ornamental candle branch. Sophie gazed with joy at the artless grandeur which was both comfortable and intimate.

'How I love the flamboyance of the eighteenth century!' exclaimed a voice behind her.

She turned to see Basilio bowing to her, handsome in his lace and velvet. For a moment, they shared a long look. Then he took her hand.

'If this morning's dress rehearsal is repeated this evening, you will be an acclaimed success, Sophia.'

'I have so enjoyed the entire experience, Basilio. I know it will end soon when you have to leave, but please let us retain our friendship.'

'That will not be possible,' he said abruptly, releasing her hand.

She began to protest, but he turned away to join his friends. Frowning, she thought his strange response must be due to anxiety about the concert.

Suddenly, a regally dressed Beth attracted her attention from the top of the small flight of stairs at the main entrance to the salon. As Sophie joined her, she said:

'Toby and I wish you to stand with us here and greet our guests, Sophie.'

Sophie smiled. 'I am honoured, Beth, and it will be my pleasure.'

'The coaches should soon be arriving. Let us first see if the twins are ready.'

They linked arms and went up to the nursery, where the rosy-cheeked twins were in costume and bursting with excitement.

'Basilio says we must perform an encore,' said Harriet, who resembled a little porcelain shepherdess.

'And are you prepared for that?' asked Beth.

'Oh, yes!' they chorused. 'Basilio taught us.'

Beth turned to Sophie. 'This concert will be Basilio's triumph; he has arranged every detail. We shall miss his presence in this house.'

Sophie nodded sadly, thinking of his inexplicable reaction to her appeal for continuing their friendship.

Toby joined them on their return to the salon.

'This is an important event, my dears,' he beamed, 'an abridgement of restraints of mourning, and you present yourselves perfectly for the occasion.' He hugged them both.

A footman approached to say that a coach was in sight, whereupon they mounted the salon stairs to the reception area. Sophie glanced back to the dais. Basilio, seated at the piano, caught her eye and smiled as he began a Haydn sonata. All is well, she thought, forming her countenance into a welcoming smile to greet the arriving guests.

The first to dawdle through the reception area were two parliamentary friends of Toby. These were followed by neighbours and their guests, until Sir Hugh and Lady Wardyne appeared, accompanied by the charming Barty who lingered alongside Sophie long after her greeting. So far, thought Sophie grimly, there was no sign of Guy or Lady Charlotte. Should they arrive together, Sophie felt she would crumple in a tremulous heap.

Suddenly, Guy appeared in the doorway. Sophie saw he had not entirely abandoned mourning-dress. A corbeau-coloured velvet coat, eminently elegant yet sombre, impressed by understatement, she thought. He looked back from whence he had entered, smiled and extended a hand for his partner. Sophie held her breath as he graciously led in the silver-haired harpist aunt of Lady Wardyne, Miss Emily Beckwith.

Toby and Beth greeted them, smiling broadly. Sophie, in a daze, bobbed a curtsy like an automaton, her eyes moistening in relief.

'We three have met before,' Guy was saying. 'I knew you would wish Miss Beckwith to share in the music feast that awaits us, Sophie, so I insisted upon escorting her . . .'

Miss Beckwith grasped Sophie's hands.

'My dear, I have you to thank for this. I could hardly believe it was happening . . .'

Sophie's eyes locked with Guy's, endeavouring to convey her admiration and gratitude. In response, Guy bent over her hand, then led Miss Beckwith away to the salon.

Sophie continued to welcome the ensuing guests with a smile more genuine than hitherto, until a red rose within a lace doily was pressed into her hand. The donor was Anton, who bowed, took up her free hand and kissed it. Nestled within the lace was a card on which was written *Sophie, mon amour, Anton.* She flushed and, seeing his partner was the over-jewelled Lady Charlotte Cotterell, countered his mocking stare with unflinching hauteur. Nothing he did or said could affect her now. They were Guy's flowers at her breast, and he had escorted Miss Beckwith to the concert because he knew Sophie would wish it. She rejoiced in the significance of these actions. Before withdrawing to the salon, Beth whispered:

'Happy, Sophie?'

'Yes,' she replied, 'you were right to wonder about Guy's consort.' Beth nodded, smiling.

After refreshments, guests returned to the salon chatting softly together until, entranced by the heady music of Mozart, Handel and

Haydn, they sat in their chairs avidly listening. At this point, Toby mounted the dais and introduced Basilio, praising his competence. Basilio announced that the concert would continue with his pupils as soloists.

Harriet and Benjie won all hearts in their serious approach and flawless presentation. Everyone rose applauding, and encores followed. Basilio sang Handel's 'Silent Worship', followed by a short tenor aria from an Italian opera. After his triumphant reception, he came to the fore to announce the performance of 'Love's Measure', which he had composed to fit words written by Miss Sophia Stapleford . . . 'who will now sing it for us.'

Basilio extended his hand and led Sophie to the piano.

'Sophia, together we shall make this this your best performance,' he whispered. 'Have trust in me.'

He had no reason to ask that of her. She trusted him without question, but there was one instruction she decided to change. She did not wish to sing her song 'to everyone'; she wished to direct it to Guy.

Among all the faces looking at her, she knew his was not there. The seat beside Miss Beckwith was vacant. Panic seized her. As Basilio's introduction started, relief surged as she saw Guy standing at the top of the salon stairs, holding the hands of Benjie and Harriet.

She could engage him by looking straight ahead, with no glance to either side. It was as she had dreamed. She began:

O dear, my dear, my sweeting,
My beau, my life, my own;
Receive your true love's greeting,
And wear it as a crown.

Sweet sovereign of my hours,
My life you have enriched,
Within your regal powers,
Your subject stands bewitched.

Your kingdom knows no measure,
Dimensions have no part,
With you is boundless pleasure,
Supreme of all my heart,
  supreme of all my heart.

There was an eerie silence after the last note faded, then everyone stood, applauding and calling for an encore. Basilio started the introduction for a repeat of the last verse. She saw that Guy and the twins were no longer on the salon stairs. This time, she thought, she would sing to all.

Guy had left the salon promptly during the ovation for Sophie. There was no doubting her message—the words echoed in his mind. He left the house and walked he knew not where until he found himself by the carriage house.

197

He could see the pony-phaeton standing inside. He entered and climbed on to the driving seat. Sitting alone in the quietude, he realized that even here he could not escape her. The reason he had purchased the carriage for the twins was due to her. Since he had become her guardian, his involvement with her had increased and was now of prime importance to him. She was supremely eligible, beautiful beyond imagination, and intelligent. He longed to court her; but in honour he dare not besmirch the relationship at this juncture. He could not respond in kind, but must keep within the narrow limits of cold and scrupulous politeness.

In truth, he could not offer anything until his own position became clear. He must anticipate ruination, which might occur should he lose the steeplechase. He sighed deeply and stretched out his hessian-booted legs, brushing specks of straw from his pantaloons. The very fact of the steeplechase depended on The Skull agreeing to Sir Henry's proposal. There was a mort to do before any possibility of a romantic attachment.

Dusk was approaching. He jumped down from the carriage and returned to the house, rehearsing reasons for his immediate departure to Adversane.

Candles were aglow in the salon, with guests sipping wine and chatting in groups. The musicians had retired for some refreshment, with the exception of the Italian tutor who was playing melodious piano pieces. Guy approached him.

'Signor Bordoni,' he said, at an appropriate pause, 'thank you for a superb recital of music. At some time in the future, I hope that you and your friends will grace my house at Adversane.'

The *signor* rose and bowed.

'It will be an honour, my lord.' He shook Guy's offered hand warmly.

Guy nodded and turned, seeking Beth and Sophie. He intercepted Beth as she broke away from a group.

'That was a wonderful event, Beth. You are to be congratulated. I must find Sophie and then Miss Beckwith, for I wish to depart immediately.'

'You are going, Guy?' said Beth, with some surprise.

'Regretfully, Beth; but I have a question. I hear that Anton has completed his task for you. How long has he stayed at Rothervale?'

'Let us go to the anteroom,' said Beth, leading the way.

The anteroom was empty of guests and Beth closed the door, 'He has been here for three weeks or so,' she replied. 'Do not fret. To my knowledge, he has not importuned Sophie—though he gave her a rose this evening, which she discarded.' There was a strained silence. Then she said quietly: 'He says he will be departing for London later with Lady Charlotte.'

'Do not leave him alone with Sophie for an instant,' said Guy with marked chill. 'He is a threat to her.'

'A threat, Guy?'

'Not only for his contumely against her person, but my naval friends think he is a Napoleonist spy. I do not wish Sophie to know this. I feel you and I are capable of protecting her.'

'Oh, Guy. I should have let you know when he arrived, but Sir Henry was your guest at that time. I'm so sorry.'

He placed his arms around her. 'Dear Beth, I do not judge you, as I did not impart the full story about Anton and the French interest in Sophie's father; but all's well, I see that.' He released her. 'Now, where is Sophie?'

'I last saw her on the terrace. Barty was hovering.'

'I must go to her.' He turned to leave, but Beth caught his arm.

'Be gentle with her, Guy. She poured her heart out to you in her song.'

He hesitated, his head bowed, then faced her and she nearly exclaimed aloud at his sudden anguished countenance.

'Oh, Beth,' he said, his voice low, 'how I yearn to crown her love with my own; but honour bids me stay until I am relieved of the guardianship—*Cautus et Audax*, remember? It

200

was father's message to me.' Beth's heart twisted for her brother, her eyes brimming. Guy continued: 'I shall embrace her as impassively as possible, and say that I wish her to return to the manor house as soon as I hear about the steeplechase. She could be of immense help.'

'That will delight her, Guy.'

'That is my purpose,' he said as he left.

CHAPTER THIRTEEN

'Anton has departed,' announced Beth the next morning over coffee. 'He dismissed his coachman and is travelling to London with Lady Charlotte.'

'She is also taking Barty,' said Sophie. 'No doubt she's pleased to be returning to London.'

'And Guy? Did you see Guy before he left?'

Sophie nodded, quietly smiling.

'He hopes that one day I shall return to the manor house to help in the steeplechase event, which means, dear Beth, I shall have to leave Rothervale some time soon. I am sad to think of this because I have been so contented here and you have helped me in countless ways.'

There was a silence as Beth drained her cup.

'There has also been another departure,

which was a complete surprise.'

'Oh?' questioned Sophie, 'and who is that?'

'Basilio—a week before I expected.'

Sophie stared at her unbelievingly.

'Basilio has gone!'

'Yes. He has returned to London with his musician friends. I had a long talk with him late last evening, Sophie. He has given me a letter for you.'

Sophie was speechless. She slumped in her chair, overcome by perplexity and the blighted hope of a continuing friendship. 'How strange,' she whispered, 'that he did not seek me to say farewell. He was very dear to me.'

'Basilio made it clear that he found himself falling in love with you, that his heart was captured and you were the warder; *ergo*, he must escape after the concert. He has behaved admirably.'

How different from Anton, thought Sophie, rising from her chair. She crossed to the window, watching the river, limpid and mirrorlike, with the squadrons of ducks sailing incessantly from one bank to the other. The ordinariness charmed her; but it could not remove a feeling of guilt. Soon she was aware that Beth had joined her, placing an arm around her shoulder.

'It is not your fault,' Beth whispered. 'Your behaviour has been admirable too, Sophie, and Basilio respected that. Here is Basilio's letter. Take it to your room and read it when you feel able.'

'Thank you, Beth.' She took the letter and withdrew from Beth's room. On the landing, she halted abruptly. She could hear piano music! Had Basilio returned? She ran down the stairs to the salon. There she saw Harriet playing merrily.

'Sophie!' she called, 'Basilio has left me lots of pieces to practise. Isn't that kind of him?'

'Very kind,' agreed Sophie, advancing to sit beside her. For me that memorable musical interlude is over, she thought.

Later, after having read and fretted over Basilio's melancholy letter, she decided to help Harriet and Benjie to establish a music-practice routine, with Beth's blessing. She felt that this was the least she could do to perpetuate Basilio's work at Rothervale.

Adversane

Within two days of his return to Adversane, Guy rode to the manor house to reassure himself that preparations for Sophie's return were proceeding. The present custodians, Mr and Mrs Parker, with the help of additional staff from Adversane, were awakening the house from its slumbers ready for the reinstatement of its young mistress. Guy was undecided as to when that should be, since it depended upon hearing from Sir Henry.

He was also anxious for news from Jack Watts and had written to him, with a degree of urgency, asking whether it was likely that Sophie's father would soon be released in a prisoner exchange; or, was it possible for the Navy soon to attempt a rescue? Guy's hopes of pursuing a deepening attachment to Sophie depended upon this; but, in his heart he knew that Jack could not convey even the slightest hint. His letter was simply a sop to his mounting need to declare his nascent feelings for Sophie, similar to those she had expressed to him in the words of her song. The only way he could justify increased involvement was to invigorate his role as guardian—hence his visit to the manor house.

When Guy later called at the stables to see Seb, he began to suspect that peripheral happenings might be significant as to the state of the steeplechase wager. Seb reported that Hynde Hallam had been joined at the Tabard by three associates, who had been exercising fine and fleet chestnut horses in the surrounding area.

'They may be from The Skull's string,' suggested Seb.

'Perhaps he's testing out the possibilities. So far as we're concerned, the challenge hasn't yet been taken up.'

'Would there be a reason to delay a formal response?' asked Seb.

'None that I can see, except a hope we could

be under-prepared.'

Seb beamed. 'We're ready at any time, my lord. It's to our advantage if he's going to use the chestnuts. They're bred for speed, whereas our greys are bred for stamina.'

Guy nodded. 'We shall have to be vigilant, none the less.' Seb's revelations troubled him. Why hadn't he heard from Sir Henry? Mindful of the preparations at the Tabard, Guy decided to proceed as if the steeplechase wager was a foregone conclusion.

Early the next morning, mounted on Japhet, he accompanied Jem as he exercised Brisket. He insisted that Jem should follow him to a likely starting-point on top of Chadlett Hill and from there pursue a route to Adversane Church. It was clear from this that it required precise knowledge of the terrain, taking account of the likely effects of the changing season. The river would be a constant hazard. There was a special person who could advise, expert in such matters from sheer experience. He must arrange for Sophie's immediate return to the manor house, and ask her to employ the skills of the girl he had seen all those months ago, riding with such splendid abandon in the dawn light.

That afternoon he decided to visit Rothervale, where he would impart the core of Sir Henry's argument and, at the same time, request Sophie's assistance.

The Manor House

Lammastide was well advanced before Sophie was again established in the manor house. The transition had been eased by Guy's hand in the arrangements, and Sophie had been warmly welcomed by the gentle Mr Parker and motherly Mrs Parker who anticipated her every need.

Sophie was happy. The atmosphere had changed from the dark shadowy time of the Lachbones and Hallam. Nell's return was welcomed with Jem's gift of a green-lined purple cloak, made by Dilly. Beth and the twins visited often, while Sir Toby, released from parliament, spent time with Guy, Seb and Squire Budge at Adversane, discussing precise plans for the race.

Sophie knew that Guy was troubled that The Skull had yet to accept his challenge. She watched and suffered with him, but encouraged and supported him in the assumption that acceptance would be forthcoming. She agreed with Sir Toby that The Skull was withholding for no good reason.

She met Guy frequently at Adversane stables, when he greeted her warmly, remaining at her side for the duration of her stay. Talk centred on Brisket's performance and features of the course; but there were shared intimate glances and the lingering touch of hands. She welcomed these encounters, for they gave her hope.

Sophie's daily rides with Jem opened her eyes and senses to the fact that summer was passing and the season advancing to Michaelmas. Odd leaves were showing rust around the edges, and some acorns were tumbling from their cups. Mantling hawthorn and bramble, she recognized the green leaf and star-like white flower of traveller's joy . . . Sophie gasped. 'Gorran', she murmured. When last she saw him, he had given her the bare twig of a creeper. *When this silvers the hedgerows, we shall return*, he had said. She drew rein, turned and guided Jet along the track to the gypsy encampment.

A blue haze of smoke beyond the copse was a hopeful sign, she thought, and wished she had brought the dogs to announce her coming. She slowed to a walk and soon she was confronted by the slight figure of Gorran standing in the road. She halted.

'I'm glad you are here, Gorran,' she said, breathlessly. 'I have not long been back at the manor house, but I need your help.'

He grinned. 'We returned just today, at noon. Well timed, my *rawnie*,' he said, withdrawing a piece of apple from his pocket and feeding it to Jet.

'There is to be a steeplechase from Chadlett Hill to the church tower on the first day of October. The earl must win it against London associates of Hallam. If he loses, then they will take over the estate. That will be a threat to you all.'

Gorran frowned. 'How can I assist in such an event?'

'Accompany me and Jem, the earl's rider, over the course and tell us how you would attempt it, Gorran.'

He smiled. 'That I will do with pleasure. I must first tell my uncle.'

'Then do so,' said Sophie, 'and if he agrees, then come with your pony to the manor house and I will take you to Jem. I cannot emphasize enough the dangers to everyone on this estate if the earl should lose.'

'His rider will ride one of the big greys?' he asked.

'Of course. It seems that Hallam, who is now staying at the Tabard . . .'

'I know where he is,' Gorran interposed, 'and who has joined him there. He has a string of chestnuts and Irish riders. There is nothing we do not know about Mr Hallam.'

Sophie realized she needed to go no further in her persuasion. She smiled, shaking her head.

'I was born here,' he added, 'this is my home.'

To Sophie's surprise, Seb and Jem appeared not to welcome Gorran to the stables, but Guy was favourably impressed with the condition of the lad's pony. After Gorran's first ride with

Sophie, Jem and Seb, from the starting point to the church by a route chosen by Jem, he pointed out that far from being a hazard, the river could provide an advantage.

'How can that be?' asked Seb, mounted on Bracelet.

'Hallam's rider will be forced to use the five bridges to cross the river. I know of three ancient crossing-places which would avoid diversion to a bridge. Come, I will show you.' So saying, Gorran turned his pony and returned to the river, followed by Sophie and the others. He halted some yards downriver and pointed to the opposite bank.

'Do you see that willow with a bulbous base almost in the river?' he said. 'It marks an ancient ford, and so long as the base is uncovered, the water there is only inches deep.' With that, he drove his pony down the bank and into the river, reaching the other side with only shallow surface splashes. Seb and Jem were dumbfounded.

'Did you say you knew of two other fords, then?' asked Jem.

'Yes, and I will show you where they are. Note them well, and do not use them again until the day of the steeplechase.'

'There's wisdom in that,' said Seb. 'When the bet is taken on, the course will be open to the others.'

Seb and Jem were pleased with Gorran's advice and returned to the stables eager to plot a new course, bearing in mind the crossings.

'Gorran, you can come here at any time,' said Seb gleefully.

The next day Gorran arrived bright and early. Again he left for the course with Seb and Jem, accompanied by Sophie.

'Several fields to the west have fences, ditches and rough going, so it's best to start out for the nearest field, Buckslea, and go through to Langlands and Tubbers,' said Gorran.

'What names are those?' Jem asked.

'The names of fields. All fields have names, the reasons are lost to memory,' said Gorran.

As Sophie had expected, Seb and Jem were again impressed with Gorran's knowledge of the locality, and Guy's gratitude was plain to see when Sophie and Seb related these things to him.

The passing of days merged into weeks. The absence of a response from The Skull was affecting Guy's initial optimism. Despite this, everything was proceeding at Adversane. Squire Budge's men would act as course stewards, while the squire managed the betting post. The entire district would be *en fête*. Guy had issued invitations to the local gentry, hunting fraternity and his London clubs. Mr Pearley, the journalist famous for reporting such events, would be coming with agents from Tattersall's and the Jockey Club. Guy invited

210

special guests to a pre-steeplechase feast to be held by him at his house, and arranged for a wooden viewing-platform to be erected.

One evening as Sophie was leaving the stables to return to the manor house, Guy stepped into her path and, catching Jet's bridle, brought her to a stop.

'Sophie,' he said. 'Guests and their ladies will be coming to my house before the start of the opening ceremony. Would you do me the honour, and give me the pleasure, of standing with me as my hostess?'

Her heart gave a lurch, and a delicious weakness born of sheer delight almost made her tumble from the saddle. 'Of course, my lord. It will be my pleasure, too.'

'It would add to *my* pleasure if you avoid the formalities and call me "Guy".' He smiled.

She nodded, her face aglow.

He took her hand, pressing it to his lips and, cupping it gently, kissed the inside of her wrist. Then, with obvious reluctance, he released her, lightly slapped Jet's flank and let her go. After a short distance, she looked back. He stood where she had left him. She waved her hand and he responded in kind before turning away.

It was in the last week of September that Guy received a copy of the bet lodged with Sir Henry and at Tattersall's. The Skull, under his name Gabriel Driscoll, would enter a horse from his stable to run against a horse from

Lord Adversane's stable. Elated, Guy thought that at last everything was falling into place.

That day, Gorran arrived with some startling news. The Tabard was teeming with horses, carriages and strangers; obviously it was the mustering point for Hallam's side. A notorious Irish rider, known as Mayo, had arrived and was seen exercising a grey which, Gorran judged, could be a sibling of Brisket's and was surely of the Adversane strain.

'That is why they withheld,' suggested Seb. 'They wanted us to believe they would enter a chestnut.'

'It will make no difference,' said Guy, 'but I wonder if they have other surprises to thrust upon us.'

Sophie retired early on the night before the steeplechase, wishing to feel rested and ready for the morrow. She planned to make an early visit to the stables, leaving Nell to prepare her gown for her debut as Guy's hostess when she returned.

It was a dark moonshine morning as Sophie led Jet from his stable to meet Jem in Buckslea field for Brisket's toning-up exercise for the race that afternoon. She had mounted Jet and started on her way to Adversane when, in the lane ahead, she saw two dim ineffectual lights each side of a dark mass which, drawing nearer, she saw was a coach slowly approaching the manor house.

She halted in surprise, whereupon the coach

stopped, the door opened and a tall authoritative figure stepped down.

'Do not be alarmed, madam. We have travelled overnight and I think we are lost. I am seeking the manor house . . .'

'You are nearby. Whom do you wish to see at the manor house?'

'Miss Sophia May Stapleford.'

'I am she,' Sophie replied, frowning. 'What is your business with me, good sir?'

By this time she could discern that the visitor was clad in the uniform of a naval officer. He was then joined by another officer from the coach. Her heart beat wildly as he said:

'We have an urgent message for you, Miss Stapleford.'

She swallowed. 'It would be best if we returned to the house, where you may deliver your message to me in conditions as prudent as they are comfortable.'

The officers bowed. 'As you wish, Miss Stapleford.'

Sophie placed Jet in charge of a groom before she returned to the house. She summoned Mr and Mrs Parker to divest the officers of their travelling clothes and afterwards show them into the captain's room, where Sophie would await them.

Lamps had been lit in the house, as daylight was tardy. Sophie stood regarding her father's portrait, hands clasped at her breast, her

213

whole being a-tremble.

'Oh, father,' she whispered, 'what news of you am I to hear?'

A soft tap on the door revealed Mr Parker, who ushered in the two officers.

'Captain Pettit and Lieutenant Summerson, Miss Stapleford,' he announced, before withdrawing.

Captain Pettit stepped forward and bowed.

'We bring good news—excellent, in fact. Your father has succeeded in making a courageous escape from France. He awaits you in London, where there are to be celebrations by reason of His Royal Highness promoting him to Vice-Admiral in recognition of his fortitude and valour.'

Sophie gasped, pressing her hands to her cheeks.

'Oh, how wonderful! Is he well? How did he escape? So many questions; but oh, I am overjoyed!'

Both officers smiled broadly.

'We shall leave your father to brief you on his escape but, suffice to say, he is in good health and anxious to see you.'

She nodded, her eyes tear-brimmed with joy; then turned away and stared out of the window where advancing brightness was banishing the gloom. That which she had awaited for years was happening—her father returned and awaiting her in London—but on this day, Guy's destiny was in question. She could not leave immediately; she had to remain at least until reassured that Jem and Brisket were well prepared for the race.

She faced the officers again, explaining she had a duty to perform before she could leave and suggested that, in the meantime, they could enjoy a hearty breakfast which Mrs Parker would be pleased to prepare for them.

'That is good of you, Miss Stapleford. However, I should emphasize that my orders are to stay this night at Weybridge, which will mean hard travelling if we are delayed.'

'I shall come to London as soon as possible. My maid Nell will accompany me on the journey, and she will make all preparations necessary for it.'

They readily acquiesced. Sophie pulled the bell-cord and instructed Mr Parker appropriately, then took her leave of the officers. Nell met her in the hall, and Sophie joyfully told her of her father's escape and the proposed journey to London. Nell embraced her and undertook to wait upon the two officers until Sophie returned to the manor house.

Lantern-lights still shone in the Adversane stables and candles burned in the windows of Seb's house. She proceeded to Buckslea, the first field after the paddocks. Jem and Brisket looked ghostly in the grey light, which was slowly giving way to the pink tinge of sunrise. They were cantering around the edge of the field, and she halted Jet to study Brisket. A wonderful gait, she thought.

Jem beckoned that he was going over the hedge to Langlands, where it was possible to give rein and gallop. He jumped the hedge in the usual place. She saw Brisket rise and clear it. Then she heard a terrible crashing sound and a cry from Jem. She rushed over to the hedge. Brisket was on his feet, but limping. Jem was lying under a tree log which had fallen upon him from a pile on the other side of the hedge.

'My leg, it's my leg,' he groaned.

'I'll get help, Jem,' she called.

She whipped through the fields and paddock, and hammered on Seb's door.

'Seb, come quickly! Brisket's injured and Jem's hurt his leg!'

Seb, cursing as he ran to the stables, saddled up a grey gelding and followed Sophie to Buckslea field. While Seb attended to Jem, Sophie caught Brisket and led him back to the stable. His front legs were injured, though not seriously, but his participation in the steeplechase later that day was now impossible.

Seb and the other grooms chaired Jem to the cottage. His leg was broken. Seb was purple with rage and gesticulating madly.

'Who dumped logs on the other side of the hedge at Buckslea!' he demanded.

'No woodman from Adversane would do it,'

said a groom.

'They weren't there afore,' said another.

'Then it was the Devil!' shouted Seb. 'The very Devil!' Sophie felt as if all life and energy were flowing out of her. 'Seb, is there another gelding ready to replace Brisket?'

He shook his head. 'Not up to his standard; but who would ride him?'

Dilly was in the bedroom making Jem as comfortable as possible. In the kitchen, Sophie and Seb stared at each other. They both realized with mounting horror that unless they could do something, the earl would lose by default.

CHAPTER FOURTEEN

Dawn was advancing, purple morning splendour melting away to gold. There were yet some hours before the race. Sophie, her thoughts in a whirl, desperately attempted to think, to seek a way out of this disaster. There flashed into her mind that her father was awaiting her! How could she leave now with this calamity threatening Guy and Adversane itself? She might be able to do something—anything, to mitigate the shame of losing by default.

She thought of Jet, wondering whether he could be an alternative to Brisket. The black gelding had belonged to the old earl, and was surely of the Adversane stable as was Brisket; but who could ride him? Who, indeed? Could she? Her dawn rides in the past were in those areas of the course. It would mean postponing the meeting with her father for several hours. She fretted, holding her head with both hands and rocking to and fro at the magnitude of the dilemma facing her. What could she do? Suddenly, she ceased all movement. Throwing caution to the wind, she decided that she could ride Jet and win for Guy. There was no choice.

Now calmer, she confronted Seb with her idea.

'Jet is tethered in the stables,' she said breathlessly. 'Let us prepare him for the race, Seb. Remove my saddle and replace it with one Jem would use.'

Seb looked ashen. 'You cannot take on this task, Miss Sophie!'

'Yes I can, Seb. I've ridden over that terrain many times, and knowing of the new crossing-places I feel certain I could meet the challenge.'

There followed a tense silence as they stared at each other. It seemed they shared an unvoiced wish to exclude Guy from the immediate worry of the accident.

'His lordship has guests,' said Seb. 'It's unlikely he will appear here and it gives us a chance to think about what's to be done.'

'The first thing to be done is to ask Dilly if

she has Jem's new cap and riding-habit to hand. If I am to do this, it's important that I wear the correct shirt in the earl's colours.'

Seb hesitated, then called to Dilly who came from the bedroom.

'I have dosed Jem with laudanum to ease his pain for now,' she said, 'but you must send one of the grooms to bring the bonesetter here, Seb.'

'That I will do', said Seb. 'Miss Sophie wants to see Jem's new habit. She's offered to take his place with Jet.'

Dilly stared at them. 'Are you mad?'

'It is the only alternative, Dilly,' said Sophie. 'Otherwise the earl will lose by default, and that will be the end for all of us.'

Dilly pondered, then nodded to Sophie.

'Come then, let's get on with it. You're of similar size to Jem, so there's not much to alter.'

Seb cautioned Sophie to await his return so that he could take her to the starting-point.

'I'll also examine Jet to see if he's in good fettle. Heaven help us!' he added.

'I cannot tell what will happen during the race, but when it's over, I should like Gorran to attend to Jet. Would you see that that is done, Seb.'

'I will,' he said, and he left to summon a groom.

She felt sick at heart that she could not stand with Guy and greet his guests, nor could she inform him of the reason why; but she was determined to prevent his knowing of the accident at this juncture. She realized, too, that she was unable to let Guy know that her father had returned; she consoled herself with the hope that his friend, Lieutenant Jack Watts, would have informed him.

By midday Dilly had tacked and stitched Jem's blue-and-white shirt to fit Sophie. Her own top-boots fitted perfectly over the breeches. She bound her hair under the black cap which was rammed tightly on her forehead.

'You'll pass; and good luck go with you, Miss Sophie,' said Dilly, hugging her.

She clung to Dilly for a moment, then turned and walked confidently to the stable, electing to remain with Jet until Seb came to lead her to the starting-point. She memorized the location of the fords—bulbous willow on the right bank, five alder-trees left bank, and towering ash with split trunk right bank; then several fields with hedges and ditches, three gates, zigzag through the copses, eventually approach the church and prepare for the huge yawner known as the Squire's Grin. She cradled Jet's head, kissed his soft nose and her hands soothed his supple back and limbs. The black coat and mane gleamed, his eyes were bright and steady.

'You are beautiful, Jet,' she whispered, 'and together we can do it.'

Seb entered the stable and locked the door behind him.

'The other side are gathering by the Chadlett starting-point. Hallam is there with a passenger in his black curricle and Mayo, their rider, is wearing a yellow shirt. Gorran was right about the big grey; it's an Adversane strain for sure. Perhaps there's an advantage in a lighter horse . . .'

'That poses a question, Seb. Are races won by the prowess of the rider or the horse?'

'Both, I should think.'

'I agree—but does familiarity with the course pose an advantage?'

'Up to a point; but Mayo is a famous rider they've engaged, skilled in the necessary assessments.'

There was a silence. Sophie had suddenly been struck by the thought that if she lost the race, Guy would be offended by her participation in something so indecorous, in conflict with the purpose of his guardianship. If she won, surely he would be appeased, and she had the distinct certainty that her father would be proud of her. This must spur her to victory, she told herself.

'There's a festal air everywhere,' said Seb, 'with fiddlers and morris-men sounding bells and rattles, carriages and people scattered all about the estate, some playing pitched games of bowls and cricket. Several races have been run on the course and there's more to come,

221

but it will clear before the final race, which is the earl's and Driscoll's.'

A light tap on the door caused Seb to unlock it, and he quickly ushered Gorran into the stable.

'Oh, your visit is so timely, Gorran,' said Sophie. 'Have you heard what has happened to Jem and Brisket?'

'There's talk about it here, my lady. I trust we gypsies are not blamed for it.'

'Hallam will accuse you, for that is his way. One has to ask oneself, who has benefited? Certainly not the gypsies.'

Gorran nodded. 'I've seen Brisket. He'll be fully recovered in a week; but Jem, not so.'

'He'll mend in time,' said Seb. 'Do you think this black gelding has the staying power, Gorran?'

'Yes, he's done it before. It's in his bones and what's around them,' answered Gorran, stroking Jet's flank. He looked up. 'I'll leave now and look for you at the finish.'

'Seb knows I wish you to attend to Jet after the race, Gorran,' said Sophie.

'Have no fears about that, my *rawnie*,' he said as he left, accompanied by Seb.

When Seb returned, mounted on Bracelet, he called to Sophie that it was time to muster for the start. She tried to banish a strange, heavy feeling of anxiety; but thought of Guy, imagining the joy in his face if she should win.

Now it was time. She led Jet out and, using

the mounting block swung easily on to his back.

'We're ready,' she said.

As she left the stables, grooms lined up to wish her well and watched her ride off to Chadlett. She kept her head down through the lanes, which were lined with people on either side. The Hallam crowd displayed some consternation as she passed. Perhaps they expected no contender after the accident to Brisket, she thought; but she rode past with growing confidence.

Flags and bunting adorned the starting-point, where stood a farm wain upon which the stewards were gathered. Mayo was in place, endeavouring to master his grey. Seb met the starters, introducing the earl's entry, and Sophie took her place, turning Jet to face the first downhill run to the course.

*　　　*　　　*

Guy accepted that Sophie might be delayed due to the unusually crowded state of the roads between the manor house and Adversane. His guests were already arriving when he found himself standing alone to greet them in the pillared reception hall of his house.

As he welcomed Sir Toby and Beth, he whispered his disappointment, having no idea what had caused Sophie's non-appearance. To

Guy's relief, Sir Toby offered to go immediately to the manor house to ascertain what had happened to her, while Beth took her place beside Guy.

A stream of faces passed in front of Guy: local faces, London faces, all mouthing wishes for his success. They moved away slowly to the salon where they took their seats and were served with oysters, venison-pie, desserts and wine. Guy, whose appetite had waned, hovered by the porch, vainly looking for Sophie's arrival. As time passed, his anxiety mounted until Beth persuaded him to consort with his guests and await the return of Sir Toby.

Guy relented and, with reluctance, joined the festivities. While engaged in earnest converse with Mr Pearley and gentlemen from the Tattersall's establishment, a footman intervened and drew Guy away before asking that he urgently attend at the stables. Guy did not hesitate and, after asking Beth to carry out duties in his place, he slipped away quietly. Frowning, he thought: nothing is going according to plan. Sophie's absence and the unusual summons from the salon did not augur well.

As soon as he left the environs of the house, he ran to the stable block where Seb was with the other grooms assembled in the yard. Seb's pallor and mumpishness were not reassuring. The words tumbling from his mouth about Jem and Brisket were as sledge-hammers, crushing Guy's hopes. There was a pause as Seb drew breath.

'Miss Sophie was there. She brought the lamed Brisket back and roused help for Jem, whose leg was broken.'

'So there's no horse running for me,' muttered Guy, his jaws clenched in grim despondency.

'Thanks to Miss Sophie, there *is* a horse running for you.'

'Then it must be the untrained Bracelet with an unskilled rider,' said Guy with defeat in his voice. Seb's expression lightened.

'No, my lord. It is Miss Sophie, wearing your colours, riding Jet, your father's black gelding.'

Guy's jaw clenched. 'Sophie on Jet!'

He knew her riding prowess. His first sight of her had been of her jumping hedges and ditches in the dawn light. Now she was risking everything for him. He must hasten to stop her, perhaps ride the race himself; but it might be too late. Devil take it! He could not stand by and allow her exposure to dangers inconceivable. He turned decisively, and snapped his fingers.

'Seb, saddle up Japhet for me and Bracelet for you. We'll get to the church quicker by the normal roadway. We must be there for her at the finish.'

Crowds slowed their progress. Men and youths were clambering over hedges, leaving vantage points from where they had seen part

225

of the race.

'Is it the grey or the black?' Seb called to them.

'We haven't seen the black, but the grey's well on the way,' they answered.

'That means Miss Sophie's on the river course,' said Guy.

Guy's feelings wavered between joy and despair. Should Sophie lose, it would fall to him to reassure her that it mattered not a jot, despite the fact of his ruination. Her direct participation as a rider in the steeplechase had never entered his mind, and he was totally unprepared as to how he should respond, whatever the result. He would rely upon his love for her.

The sun had passed its zenith for that day and would sink in autumnal glory. Were his days at Adversane approaching their nadir? Every yard he galloped brought him nearer to the unknown fate awaiting him.

The journey to the church seemed interminable. Huge crowds were gathered at the finishing post. Seb rode ahead, clearing the way for him.

*　　*　　*

As soon as Mayo appeared in control of his mount, the starting-flag came down. Sophie, her mind implanted with the route and its characteristics, ignored the shouting as she guided Jet to the side and galloped down along the hedgerow to the first stubble field, then flat out uphill, increasing pace. Jet took a ditch in his stride, but ahead wooden rails loomed large. He shortened his stride and measured with cocked ears the distance to the take-off. They sailed through the air, Sophie glimpsing the rails beneath before a perfect landing. She caught sight of Mayo's yellow shirt to the left. He was going round to the bridge, while she was forging ahead to the riverbank, through an open gate, now down to the first ford with minimum stride and little splashing.

Suddenly, she decided she had made a mistake in keeping the saddle on Jet—it inhibited her prowess. For this type of riding, she was unused to a saddle. She reined in, leapt off and, fingers trembling, quickly unbuckled and dumped the saddle in a thicket. Standing upon a fallen tree trunk, she grasped Jet's mane and was about to remount, when she looked back at the sound of pounding hoofs approaching. It was Mayo—she could hardly believe it. He stormed by, scattering the dead leaves on the track and let fly his whip at her; but she dodged behind a tree.

'Oi'll ride ye down! Oi'll ride ye down!' he snarled. The threat in his action and his words left her angry and defiant. She knew she had lost time and the advantage of the first ford. Could she push Jet to the limit? It had been some time since they had shared those wild gallops. She remounted. Now she had effective leg control, she galloped Jet in the wake of Mayo and soon caught sight of him floundering in a marshy copse, shouting and employing his whip violently on the grey. She felt vindicated in seeing his plight, and set Jet to a fast gallop, overtaking Mayo by using a solid pathway well-known to her.

She whirled through a small copse, where a low branch snapped back and hit her right cheek but, unconcerned, she kept her pace, crashing through undergrowth and ducking under trees with trailing fronds. Mayo was nowhere to be seen, so she sought the riverbank to look for the group of alders and the second ford. Here she panicked. She had come too far down river and could not recognize the crossing-place. Sweat was beginning to fleck Jet's neck; there was no time to go back. She slowed, trying to find a narrow spot to attempt a jump. A broad bank tempted her, and she drove Jet forward to the flow. He rose, jumped short, drenching them both, and scrambled up the opposite bank in a mass of splashes and spray. As they crossed a fallow field, exuding water drops, clods of earth rose in their wake, leaving her legs caked in mud. She used her hand to wipe away a wetness from her cheek, thinking it to be water from the river crossing, but red streaks indicated bleeding scratches from the branch that had hit her face.

Suddenly she saw Mayo galloping across the fallow field she had just left. She urged Jet forward to a stubble field, full of tussocks, twitch and thistles. She guided Jet to the narrow sward near the hedge, but Mayo crossed diagonally and came up in full gallop behind her. She had a slight edge on him; but he was shouting and using his whip again. He was right on her heels; it seemed he really was intending to ride her down.

She darted away and dived through an opening into a small field where there was a large company of moles, their earthy piles hiding soft holes—a danger: they had toppled a king. She quickly escaped by plunging through the hedge on to a sunken lane, and was happy to see Mayo, who had committed himself to crossing the field, ensnared in the mole hills.

She approached the last crossing of the river by jumping over the crumbling walls of a ruined farmhouse, leading down to an open bank. Again, haste denied her recognition of the ash with the split trunk, there were many similar trees on that stretch. Further along the bank she knew there was a stone bridge but in approaching it, she saw the river narrowed sufficiently for Jet to jump it. The bank was clear enough to give him a good run, and he soared over the river with ease, then, on landing, snorted, tossing his head and shaking off the foam around his mouth. She had to hasten to stay ahead of Mayo, and kept to diagonal crossing of fields, startling grazing cattle and dealing with half-open gates. Her eyes were smarting from specks of straw and grit, and it was through a moist mist that she saw the ground rising to the final hazard, the Squire's Grin.

At that moment her right rein slackened alarmingly. She saw with horror the broken link of control between her guiding hand and Jet's bit! The only way to deal with this was to summon all her skills and repose her trust in Jet. Jet veered to the left. She grasped his mane with her right hand.

'Come right, Jet!' she commanded, tugging. 'We're nearly there!' Jet responded, turning to her will.

Looking back, she saw a flash of bright yellow emerging from the valley. It was Mayo. All her instincts for tackling the yawner were abandoned as the broken rein flapped uselessly. She had to leave the attempt entirely to Jet. He rose and, in a wide arc, cleared the yawner; but in the final dash to the finish she could hear Mayo cursing and beating up the hill behind her. Again, he attempted to come alongside but she strove for that extra effort from Jet—she thought his heart would burst, and hers break—but their unity of purpose, an exultation of shared determination, carried her first past the post with Mayo storming no more than half a length behind.

She continued on at speed until Gorran, mounted on his pony, managed to stop her. He had seen the broken rein.

The earl's blue-and-white flag was raised and cheers rang out from the crowds gathered near the betting-post, where the jubilant Squire Budge was dancing a jig. Sophie lay along Jet's back, conscious of the warm vapour rising from his body. She fell forward with her arms around his neck, her eyes filling with tears. Jet was sweat-dampened, foaming and breathing heavily with nostrils flared, but Gorran produced a hemp-palm rug and straw, and prepared to lead Jet away.

'You've won, my *rawnie*,' he said, grinning.

Sophie, overcome by nervous exhaustion, slowly collapsed and dropped from Jet's back into the many strong arms that were there in readiness to catch her.

*   *   *

Shouts and applause greeted Guy's arrival as Squire Budge came forward with both hands extended. Guy was still unaware of the result.

'What a rider! What a horse!' the crowd chorused.

'Came in like a black arrow from the east,' someone said.

Guy turned to Seb and extended his hand.

'It seems congratulations are in order,' he said, his voice trembling.

'The devil they are!' was the relieved rejoinder.

The squire led them to Jet, in Gorran's charge.

'Take good care of him, Gorran,' Guy said softly.

'I will, my lord.' Guy turned again to the squire.

'Where is Miss Sophie?' The squire looked surprised by his question.

'My lord, were you not aware of the coach and the two gentlemen who have taken her to London?'

'Taken her to London,' repeated Guy in shock.

'Her maid and the gentlemen escorted her to the coach. It was so timely, I thought you had arranged it,' said the squire.

Guy let fall an oath. 'I knew nothing of this,' he said in anguish, with an overwhelming desire to be with Sophie to assist in her recovery from the formidable race. Suddenly, a dreadful thought struck him. He wondered if Anton had had a hand in this. Could she have been taken under his instructions? All the warnings from Jack Watts gathered in Guy's mind; he should have been more vigilant. People were pressing round to congratulate him; but he could not rejoice with them.

Squire Budge frowned. 'If it's of any help, my lord, the gentlemen appeared to be in naval uniforms. Would it be anything to do with her father?'

'Are you certain?' demanded Guy.

'Yes,' said the squire, backed up by others standing near. Guy's initial dread ebbed away. It might well be to do with her father. A propitious return, he thought.

Reassuring the squire, he told Seb he would return to the house by way of the steeplechase course. Giving rein, he challenged the hazards, not to exult in his success but to vent his chagrin at being deprived of sharing it with Sophie. Her presence would have been paramount to him; the victory was hollow without her. A gnawing grief assailed him; he would not rest until he knew the circumstances of her sudden departure for London.

After handing Japhet to a groom, he entered the house. The first person he saw waiting in the hall was Sir Toby, who displayed obvious relief at his appearance.

'Guy, Mr and Mrs Parker have told me all that has happened. As Sophie was leaving the manor house this morning, a coach arrived with two naval officers, Captain Pettit and Lieutenant Summerson, enquiring for her. In the captain's room she was told the wonderful news that her father had escaped and awaited her in London. In spite of that, she chose to make a quick visit to the stables to see Jem and Brisket. The officers agreed to wait, being assured she would soon return. Breakfast was served to them by Mrs Parker, but as time passed, the officers showed impatience. They had orders to reach Weybridge by nightfall. Mrs Parker consulted with Nell, and they prepared Miss Sophie's necessaries for the journey . . .' Toby paused.

'Go on, Toby!' said Guy, urgently.

'They could wait no longer, and it was Nell who suggested they get ready and go to the finishing-point at the church. Her instincts were right, for we now know what happened to Sophie and that she won the steeplechase for you and Adversane!'

Guy stood for some moments with head bowed. Then he looked up.

'Thank you, Toby,' he said. 'Your words are the best I have heard all day.' They clutched each other. 'Toby, please arrange the payment details of the bet on my behalf. Do whatever is necessary. I am leaving immediately for London.'

'Now? Alone?'

'Yes, mounted on Japhet.'

'It's highwayman-time, so pack your pistols. Why not wait until tomorrow, Guy.'

'I cannot delay another second. Her father's freedom is by way of a release for me. The restrictions imposed by the guardianship are no more. I must seek the admiral with all speed to declare my deep love of his daughter and offer for her hand in marriage. She is my ideal, the most adorable in existence. I want her by my side. I shall plead for the admiral's favour to that end.'

Toby's face was wreathed in smiles. 'Go forth and win her, Guy,' he said.

CHAPTER FIFTEEN

She was aware of hands cradling her, lifting her high, and cheers resounding from all directions. Suddenly, Nell was there supporting her, removing her riding-cap and wrapping a hooded cloak around her. The two naval officers handed her into the coach, plumping the squabs for her comfort. Apologies flowed that they had to leave immediately without ceremony, since the drive would be long and hard. Sophie had no strength left to demur and yielded in a daze. She lay against the well-padded back seat of the coach, holding Nell's hand and attempting to reassure her about Jem—'He's in Dilly's care . . .'

Converse lapsed as the coach picked up speed. Sophie napped as well she might; but images from the steeplechase blazed in her mind, her darling Jet, spent and weak, the malevolence of Mayo, autumn's hand on the woods and fields and, lastly her triumph, strangely deficient without Guy's presence. She imagined his delight at the outcome, and yearned to see him; but that for which she had prayed all these years was now happening—her father's return from France. He was waiting for her in a Grosvenor Square apartment!

The night journey seemed never-ending. A single lantern lit the entrance to the Warren Arms at Weybridge and, in the dim light, Sophie was surprised to see several coaches in the yard which had just arrived or were departing. Ostlers swarmed around them, while porters attended the passengers.

She was shown into a comfortable upper room with a large bed upon which she lay prostrate, indifferent to its hardness. Her head and limbs ached from the long lurching drive and the respite was indeed a benison. Sleep came in snatches, but it sufficed.

She rose refreshed at Nell's welcome arrival to dress her in a beige travelling-dress and brown velvet spencer. The thorn-jagged berry-stained clothing she had worn for the race had been discarded. There was one scratch from the steeplechase still evident high on her cheek, but Nell's expert dressing of her hair concealed it.

Captain Pettit and Lieutenant Summerson greeted her warmly at breakfast in the dining-salon, politely remarking on her transformation. Sophie smiled to herself. The steeplechase had been won; now she was ready for the admiral and London.

The sights, sounds and smells of London at

once pleased and dismayed her. Roads thronged with wheeled vehicles slowed their progress. On every side there was tumult, steaming horses, shouting coachmen.

'How can you live with the noise, and crush of people and carriages,' marvelled Sophie. The two officers laughed.

'We feel as you do when we return from long sea-duty. It's an acquired taste, Miss Stapleford. The pleasures of London far outweigh its disadvantages. I'm sure you will find it so,' said Lieutenant Summerson.

'I'm sure I shall,' Sophie replied. She leaned back on the cushions. 'I am happy that you report my father is well.'

'He arrived from Portsmouth only yesterday and did not wish to delay your reunion. He wants you to share in all the celebrations in his honour,' said Captain Pettit.

Sophie smiled. 'I cannot put words to the pleasure it will give me to do so.'

The coach drew up outside an elegant mansion facing the green in Grosvenor Square. Sophie entered the house on the arm of Captain Pettit, followed by Nell and Lieutenant Summerson. Mrs Florence Pettit, her ribboned cap rustling in her haste to please, received them in the hall. It appeared the admiral's callers had by now left the house and he was awaiting his daughter in the main salon. Mrs Pettit ushered Sophie into a luxurious pillared room where a tall bed, curtained in cerise and pale green, took pride of place.

Sophie threw herself on to the bed with a sigh of relief that the journey was over. Some moments later she rose to inspect the closet's facilities. She wanted to look her best for her father without a hint of fatigue to mar the occasion, and was grateful to Nell for packing all her necessaries for the journey. After a refreshing ablution, she selected a gown of grey-blue jaconet and a velvet spencer, pinning her mother's sapphire brooch to the lace chemisette at her bosom. Nell assisted with a final adjustment to her hair before she was ready to meet her father.

Captain Pettit escorted her to the salon, pushed open the double doors and announced her presence.

The familiar lean figure in the frock uniform of an Admiral of the Blue, turned from the window and Sophie, with a cry of joy, ran to him. He came towards her, holding out his arms, and clasped her to his breast.

'My dear, dear girl,' he gasped. 'How lovely you are! Oh, I've dreamed of this moment.'

He held her at arm's length, then again drew her close.

'I, too, have dreamed of it; but it's better by far than any dream to have you home again,' she whispered, her eyes moist.

He led her to a sofa. 'Let me look at you,' he said, his eyes seeming unable to leave her face. 'You are well? Not too tired after your journey? I must remain in London for a short time before returning to Adversane, but I could not resist sending for you.'

'But are *you* well?' she asked. 'You've met so many dangers and you appear untouched by them.'

'I am never untouched by danger, rather I am constantly reminded of it in giving thanks for deliverance. Once or twice I feared for my life, but was no more exposed to sudden death than the riders in Hyde Park at five o'clock or any pedestrian on the streets of London.'

Sophie smiled. 'So the wide open sea is safer, more desirable?'

'Until now. All I wish is a quiet country life with my daughter nearby. Now, tell me about Adversane, the new earl, and everything,' he said briskly, clasping her hands in his. 'I have so many questions. Are you prepared for that?'

'I will relate all with pleasure but you will grow weary before I cease. Are you prepared for that?'

He nodded, rose and pulled a bell-cord, whereupon a footman entered.

'We wish to take refreshment here. This table will be sufficient for the purpose.' Turning again to Sophie, he continued: 'You have had much to endure in the journey, so we shall eat and talk here until all is said that must be said after so long an absence.'

Sophie sighed with happiness.

Soon, they were able to recruit themselves on the viands, wine and coffee served by the staff. As her father questioned her intimately about the changes the new earl had wrought in her life, Sophie smiled. She talked animatedly of the earl's virtues, and her affection for other members of his family. She stopped herself from mentioning the steeplechase and her part in it, reasoning that that would come later, much later, when they were back at Adversane. Their converse continued until candles were lit in the salon and lamplighters were on their rounds in the square.

The admiral rose and poured two glasses of wine. Both sipped in silence until Sophie said:

'Now you must tell me what is planned for your accolade.'

'There have already been certain functions at Portsmouth and next month more will follow at Greenwich; but the most important takes place in four days' time. Despite the lateness of the Season, His Royal Highness is cognizant of those returning from long service in the wars, and he is leaving Brighton for a short sojourn in town especially to grant military and naval awards. We have been invited to attend as guests of the Prince Regent at a reception in Carlton House.'

'Oh, Father!' she cried, hugging him in delight. Suddenly, she gulped. 'But—I have no ball-dress, certainly not for a Court occasion.'

'All is in hand. Tonight when you disrobe, a flotilla of Court modistes will attend you under the guidance of Mrs Pettit and Lady Adela Summerson. Those officers' ladies have attended such affairs in the past and will be of help to you.'

'Is it possible that a ball-dress will be ready in time?'

'My dear, this is London. There are many talents here able to work miracles through the night. Tomorrow they will wait upon you to fit the dress and all that goes with it.'

'Then I should retire now, to give more time to the willing hands, Father.'

He rose and escorted her to the door. Embracing her, he said:

'Goodnight, my dear. I am truly proud of you.'

She smiled, kissing him lightly.

The admiral watched her walking briskly to her room. He quietly closed the salon doors and opened his sea-chest, withdrawing paper and writing-materials. He placed a branch of candles on his desk, wrote a long letter, sealed it and summoned a footman.

'I wish this letter to be delivered immediately. If there is no one in residence at the address, return with the letter unopened,' he said, handing it to the footman.

The admiral sighed, crossed to the window and, drawing aside the curtains, stood looking over the square. For some time he regarded

241

the glowing windows of the elegant houses. Steeple bells chimed the hour as the admiral glanced below and saw the departure of the ladies who had called to measure Sophie for her ball-dress. It was midnight.

The staff entered to attend the wax-lights in the salon. The admiral snuffed out the candles in the branch on his desk, bade the staff a fair night and withdrew to his bedroom.

The next morning brought many callers to the house. Naval officers and Members of Parliament kept the admiral busy with official matters. The sequence of events that day permitted only limited glimpses of his daughter, surrounded as she was by the ladies, modistes and sempstresses.

That evening they dined in company with Captain and Mrs Pettit and Lieutenant and Lady Adela Summerson, who regaled them with anecdotes of other royal gatherings they had attended. As dusk fell and candlelight flooded the salon, they retired to rest in preparation for the morrow's activities.

The admiral was particularly pleased. The footman who had delivered his letter the previous evening had returned with a hastily written response from its recipient who had, at that late hour, barely arrived in London. His reply contained the words:

. . . so great an honour to be invited thus, outweighed only by the joy of witnessing the

242

happiness of Miss Stapleford. In order to aid your conspiracy of surprise, I shall endeavour patiently to await the royal event before making my presence known. In so doing, I wish you to know that this is the most difficult order with which you request I comply. For too long I must withhold my homage to you for your honour and promotion and to your daughter for her beauty and talent. Sir, I shall do so with as much fortitude as I can muster . . .

There followed the signature: *Adversane.*

Guy had arrived unexpectedly at his London house on the cusp of midnight, to the consternation of his housekeeper and carriage-house staff. His journey from Adversane had been tiring and mercifully uneventful. He had followed Sir Toby's advice to abandon his plan to ride off on Japhet unaccompanied, and delay for sufficient time for the coach to be readied so that he could travel with Lewis and a groom.

He retired to his bedchamber soon after his arrival, but was roused by a hammering upon the door. It was a footman delivering a letter which, after reading, demanded an immediate response. He lit a candle in the porter's room off the main hall and wrote his answer, giving it to the footman, who walked away briskly into the shadows. He was about to close the door when a hushed whisper from the side of the porch forced him to admit Lieutenant Jack Watts.

'No social call this, Guy,' he said, as Guy quickly shut the door. 'Our French *comte* has revealed his hand and the threat to Miss Stapleford is real.'

'Come in here, Jack,' said Guy, stepping back into the porter's room, 'and tell me all you know.' The candle-flame fluttered as they both sat at the table.

'We have learned that the *Comte* is to sail to Ostend and will board a London-to-Gravesend stagecoach. We believe he will stay at the Bull, Dartford, which is a stage-stop on the way to Gravesend.'

'That's good news. He's out of the way, so let him proceed,' said Guy.

'But all is not well. I have been warned by my Bourbon counterpart that they are interested in the activities of this *comte*. He is a disaffected *émigré* who has solicited promise after promise on the pretext of support, but there is a possible duplicity in loyalty. Further, he has no mission for the Bourbons in Belgium and it is thought he will be returning to France.'

'How does this affect Miss Stapleford, Jack?'

'It is said he was breathing revenge against the admiral for escaping, thus wrecking French hopes of a prisoner exchange. Of his own volition, he may attempt to abduct Miss Stapleford and hold her, pending resumption of the negotiations that were abandoned. If successful, he is counting on the restoration of his estates in Poitiers.'

Guy rose in such anger that his chair fell with a crash and the solitary candle dipped and danced. Choked with rage, he shouted:

'Arrest him, Jack! Arrest him!' He punched the palm of one hand with the fist of the other. 'Oh, how I grieve that it was under my auspices that he met her!'

Jack rose and faced him. 'We can arrest him for any move he makes against Miss Stapleford. Meanwhile, we are keeping a watch on her comings and goings. So far, she is well-escorted by her father, Captain Pettit and Lieutenant Summerson.'

'Then continue, Jack. Keep me closely informed and permit me to be included in your activities to protect her.'

Jack readily agreed, upon which they shook hands. Guy extinguished the candle and watched Jack depart into the darkness.

He slept little, tossing and turning, his mind in turmoil. More than anything, he wanted to be by Sophie's side, to let her know he was nearby; but it was necessary to respect the admiral's conspiracy of secrecy and appear as his guest at Carlton House. He was counting the hours to their reunion. He rose late the next morning, and consulted with Lewis about his Court dress for the occasion.

He called in at his club for a late breakfast, then took a hackney to a jewellers' in Holborn. Dark clouds sailed across the sky and, as he returned to the house, rain was steadily falling. In the library, Jack Watts was pacing the floor.

'Come, Guy. You are needed,' he said crisply.

Guy hastened to action. He changed into his riding-habit, borrowed one of his neighbour's horses as a mount, took up his sword-cane and prepared his Manton pistols, knowing he would challenge Anton should the opportunity arise. Confident and determined, he thought of those golden words in his father's portrait at Rothervale: *Cautus et Audax*. Now it was time for boldness.

*   *   *

Sophie was nervous and uncertain as to Court etiquette, and found it of comfort to know that Captain and Mrs Pettit were included in the admiral's party. She was assured that as soon as the royal presentations were over, she could withdraw and enjoy the convivial company of her father, his colleagues and young officers, who would no doubt be competing to attend her.

The ball dress was beginning to take shape. It was obligatory for Court functions that the skirt be hooped, that the gown have a train

246

and that ostrich feathers adorn the head-dress. Sophie, summoned for fittings morning and afternoon, was looking for a moment to slip away and purchase a gift for her father to celebrate his return.

The opportunity arose in the late afternoon of the second day. With Nell, bonneted and cloaked, she ordered the coach to take them to the shop offering silver and plate in the Strand, as recommended by Lady Adela. Crowds obstructed their progress and it was some time before the coach drew up outside the premises.

'Nell, I suggest you remain in the coach while the coachman drives on to turn round,' said Sophie, 'and I shall look for you over there.' She pointed to a place opposite. 'That will save time. I know what I wish to order, so I will be back in an instant.'

Sophie was escorted into the shop by a uniformed attendant, ushered to a chair and treated with the utmost courtesy as she ordered a pair of silver wine-glass coolers, each engraved with nautical scenes. Early delivery was assured and, happy with her achievement in so short a time, she promptly left the shop.

The sky had darkened, heralding rain. The pavement was so crowded that, for a moment, she was hustled along in a direction she did not wish to go. She turned abruptly to escape the throng, at the same time looking for a sight of Nell and the coach across the road. Neither was there.

Suddenly she saw a figure in a green-lined purple cloak waiting by a carriage a short distance away. Assuming the woman to be Nell, she hastened towards it but, before she could inspect the crest upon the door, she was roughly bundled into the coach.

'In yer go, milady!' shrieked the cloaked figure and, gesticulating to the coachman aloft, shouted: 'Drive on, ye dolt of a jarvey!'

Sophie, looking back, was startled to see the purple hood fall back, and a straw-haired wench with a pockmarked face and black teeth slapping herself with uncontrolled mirth.

'There's a mistake!' Sophie cried. 'This is not my coach! Coachman! Stop!'

She called out again and again, but the coachman ignored her cries and proceeded at breakneck speed through courtyards and backways until the crowded streets were left behind. Her entreaties were lost in the thundering wheels and scudding hoofs of the horse.

Breathless, she sat back and ordered her thoughts. At first she felt she must be the victim of a genuine mistake but, as the journey progressed, she began to doubt. The coachman, ignoring her pleas, was taking her to some destination; but where? What had happened to Nell? She was certain the woman was wearing Nell's cloak.

She cleared a spot on the grimy window and through the murk she saw that rain was falling. Not a light could be seen. She reasoned they had crossed the river over Westminster Bridge and must now be in Southwark. She had been told that this place harboured rogues who nightly propelled boats over the river to cause mayhem in the City. Travellers were under threat here, and their pace indicated the coachman was aware of it.

Later, looking through the window again, she saw the rain-clouds had vanished. The yellow murk had given way to fingers of mist. Tracks were visible, vanishing into the darkness of what seemed copses and fields. Her anxiety grew as the coach proceeded into areas of which she had no knowledge.

She sat clutching the edge of the seat, despite the rocking lurch of the coach. They must soon arrive at a hostelry for a change of horses, and she looked to that moment for a chance to elude the coachman. For some time she remained thus until she became aware of another sound coming from behind. Pounding hoofs were rapidly gaining upon the coach and she heard shouts of 'Halloa!' and 'Hold to!'.

The coachman was using his whip in a frenzy as a rider, flinching under the lashes, passed at speed and leapt upon the coach-horse. The coach bowled on out of control until skilfully drawn to a halt. Sophie saw the coachman leap from the box and attempt to escape, but he was caught by a man with a flambeau who had appeared out of the darkness with other riders.

Sophie, about to belabour the window, was relieved when the door opened.

'Miss Stapleford,' said a gentle voice, 'there has been a terrible mistake. You boarded the wrong coach and I am commissioned to return you to your father immediately. Lieutenant Jack Watts, at your service.'

'Oh,' she said. 'I believe you are a friend of Lord Adversane.'

'Indeed, I am,' he replied, helping her from the coach and escorting her to another carriage that had quietly approached from the other direction. 'We were alerted by your maid. My colleagues shall be your outriders back to London.'

Sophie settled back on the cushions, her heart still racing and thoughts in a whirl. The lieutenant's explanation was all too simple. She felt sure she had been the victim of an attempted abduction. The rider who had given chase and stopped the coach so adroitly had disappeared into the night. Who was he whose actions had thwarted the intention?

She pondered deeply on the circumstances of the incident, failing to find a reason for it, and regretting her lack of opportunity to question the coachman.

On arrival at Grosvenor Square, she was immediately taken to the admiral and, after embracing her and raising some questions, he appeared to agree that she had been the victim of a gross misunderstanding. Nell, on seeing Sophie safely returned, hugged and assured her that she was still in possession of her cloak.

Taking an evening repast with her father, Sophie felt reassured by his dismissal of the event as of no consequence, and then engaged her fully with vivid details of his treatment in the French prisons.

As she left to retire, the admiral watched her enter her room. He then summoned Captain Pettit to ascertain the facts in the report given to him by Lieutenant Jack Watts. They discussed it at length, and the admiral concluded by saying gravely:

'I do not wish to curtail my daughter's activities Captain Pettit; but it may be advisable for the time being that she be accompanied by you or Lieutenant Summerson on any future excursion beyond these walls.'

CHAPTER SIXTEEN

After Guy had stopped the coach carrying Sophie, his undertaking to the admiral behoved him to withdraw from the scene, which he found contrary to all desire and reason; but he was won over when he saw her safely in the Royal Navy coach on the way back to her father, with outriders in attendance.

Jack had assigned him an important task— to question the coachman as to his destination. First he had to find his horse, which had continued galloping on. He hailed his colleague with the flambeau to light his way, and it was some yards ahead that they found the bay gelding nibbling the grass sward by the roadside. He mounted and returned to the copse where the coachman had been apprehended by others of the party. Guy saw that the old man was only too willing to reveal all, in the hope that he would be released.

'It was a French gemmun, my lord, paid for a single fare to the Bull at Dartford—a bit o' petticoat—er, a young lady, my lord.'

'Then to the Bull we shall go,' said Guy. 'Here's a guinea for the use of your coach and your caped coat. There'll be another guinea for you in its pocket when you collect both at the Bull.'

The coachman brightened, tugged his forelock, and took off into the wood. Guy was joined by Jack Watts.

'We'll drive the coach to the Bull,' said Guy, 'and I will be its passenger. Instead of the lady he expects, our French friend will have a surprise.'

'Do not take undue risks, Guy,' cautioned Jack.

252

'It's a matter of honour between us. I'll roast that bird.'

A feeling of renewed purpose possessed him. He was surprised at Anton's impudence in planning such an escapade and acknowledged the guile of his stratagem. It could be regarded as a typical coach muddle. Anton would await a confused and anxious Sophie at the Bull, with his the one familiar face, ready to promise help. A tincture of laudanum in a cup of cheer and Sophie would be helpless on her way with him to Ostend, and thence to France. Jack hailed the man with the flambeau.

'Fitch! You know how to drive a coach. Here's a job for you.'

Fitch grinned. 'Yes, sir. Where to, sir?'

'To the Bull at Dartford, with myself as your passenger,' said Guy.

Fitch doused the flambeau in a ditch before throwing it away, then walked over to the coach and tended its patient, blinkered horse.

'I've heard the Bull is a busy place,' said Jack, 'with coaches coming and going all the time; but our *comte* is no doubt keeping a watch for this one from London.'

'So I have reasoned. He'll be aware of our arrival, but I have been trying to outguess his contrivance. There are two ways for him to make the approach to his supposed captive. One is that he will come directly to the coach, whereupon my challenge will be lodged there

253

and then; but my feeling is that he will employ cunning to win the confidence of our lady and disarm her panic by having her conducted to a room at the Bull. In that case, I shall play his game with him.'

'God give strength to your purpose, Guy,' said Jack, shaking his hand.

Fitch, now garbed in the coachman's caped coat, clambered aloft while Guy climbed inside the coach and settled back out of sight in the darkness.

The night was drear. The palely flickering lamps each side of the coach served only to denote its presence rather than shed light on the way. At the dreaded Shooter's Hill, they took hold of the horse and urged the equipage up the tortuous hill; then aided a safe descent through the wooded and misty downside.

After many miles they saw houses lining the road at the approach to Dartford, with candlelights flickering here and there. In the town, cloaked figures stood back to let them pass through the narrow thoroughfares. They entered the Bull through an archway off the street and came to a stop in the courtyard. Apart from a parked curricle, there were no other coaches to be seen, but the lower rooms of the inn were ablaze with light, and staff were active inside and outside the premises.

Two ostlers came running.

'Are ye from Lunnon?' one called to Fitch.

Fitch nodded, at the same time flinging

down the reins in the manner of regular coachmen.

'Is there a bit o' skirt on board?'

'Aye.'

At this one of the ostlers darted off and returned with a maid-servant. Guy, watching from the window, judged her to be a simple country wench, tipped to perform a duty.

'My lady?' she called at the window. Hearing no answer, she opened the coach door and leaned inside. 'My lady, a room is available for your comfort and rest. Come with me, I'll take you to it and bring you a mite of refreshment besides.'

Guy, swathed and muffled in his cloak and hood, cowered his way into the inn on the arm of the maidservant, who led him to an upper room overlooking the courtyard. He heard the key turn in the lock as she left. He had no doubt that Anton would soon present himself. Guy sat in a chair by a desk, placing himself with his back to the room. He withdrew the blade from his sword-cane.

He had not long to wait. The key turned, the door quietly opened, closed, and the latch caught again. There was a pause, then an exclamation of surprise.

'*Mademoiselle!* This room is reserved for me. I fear there has been a mistake.'

It was Anton. Guy rose to his feet and cast off his cloak with dashing speed. He turned, his small-sword dancing at Anton's throat.

255

'*Your* mistake, Anton. She whom you expected is safely with her father.'

A pallor crept over Anton's face as Guy forced him back towards the door.

'Guy . . .' he spluttered. 'I can explain.'

'My name cannot be used by you in friendship ever again. *Here it ends!*' As further emphasis, the tip of Guy's small-sword deftly disjoined Anton's stock and cast it at his feet. 'I call upon you to give me that satisfaction for your conduct which a gentleman has a right to require,' he continued.

Anton smiled, still sickly pale.

'I am not armed . . .'

'Then, demme, sir . . .'

A thunderous hammering at the door stopped Guy's violent utterance. Loud voices demanded admission.

'Who's there!' shouted Guy, striding to the door and flinging it wide.

Lieutenant Summerson stepped into the room, followed by the landlord of the Bull and two naval petty officers.

'My Lord Adversane,' said Lieutenant Summerson, acknowledging Guy. 'I have a warrant for the detention of Count Anton-Alexandre de Saint-Gabriel by authority vested in me by the Lords of Admiralty and the House of Bourbon.'

Anton laughed softly.

'Thwarted, Guy. It's as well, for the satisfaction you seek is obviously political and

256

not, as I thought, that we both desire the lovely Miss Stapleford.'

'The political aspects are unknown to me. They are a separate matter.' Turning to Lieutenant Summerson, Guy continued: 'Summerson, delay your arrest until I have the satisfaction of a duel of honour. You cannot refuse me.'

Lieutenant Summerson considered for a moment.

'If you desire a duel of honour, you will forbear at this juncture,' he said. 'At daybreak, we shall retire to a field at the back of the inn and there the duel will be carried out, under supervision, in an orderly and proper manner, with seconds. Gentlemen, I presume you have agreed as to weapons.'

'Pistols,' Anton said, without hesitation.

'Do you agree, my lord? I have with me a brace of pistols primed for use. You are both welcome to them.'

'Then pistols it will be,' said Guy, as he strode towards the door. Turning to the landlord, he requested the use of a room on another floor until the appointed hour.

After being shown to an apartment, he threw himself on the settle. He was angry. The interruption of his challenge had irritated him. The core of his quarrel with Anton was his abduction of Sophie. He cared little about Anton's political motives, but he felt obliged to subdue his vengeful feelings and co-operate with Lieutenant Summerson.

He called a waiter and ordered a cup of chocolate, eggs and whisky to fortify him. He had been told that this was excellent for steadying the hand before a duel. He then penned a letter to Sophie for delivery should he fall in the duel. Affirming his love, he devised to her various gifts of preferment from his most precious possessions at Adversane, should such circumstances arise. He wrote other letters to the admiral, Beth, Toby and the children. He lay on the bed, slumbering at intervals, awaiting the dawn.

At sunrise, he took another swig of the bolstered chocolate before leaving his room and, taking the letters with him, he made his way to find Summerson and ask him to ensure their delivery if and when appropriate. In the greying light, he could see the courtyard was still busy and that there were many tapers in the public rooms.

He was crossing the yard when suddenly a voice from behind hailed him. It was Jack Watts with Fitch. Both were mounted.

'Your bird has flown, Guy,' said Jack. 'Showing his true colours, he escaped the night guard and made off to Gravesend.'

'He has absconded?'

'That was his intention; but Summerson caught up with him, and he has been arrested.'

'Where is he now?'

'On his way to prison in London.'

Guy sighed deeply. 'Even to the end, he acted dishonourably. He is contemptible.'

'A debased gentleman,' added Jack. 'The rescue party has been disbanded. We will return with you to London, and have brought your bay horse safely to the stable here.'

'Let us meet in the dining-room for a substantial repast before we leave,' said Guy. 'I am well disposed to ale for breakfast on some mornings, and this happens to be one of them!'

He briefly returned to his room, lit a fire in the grate and burned the letters he had written. Before his departure, he visited the site at the back of the Bull where the duel had been arranged. He saw a pleasant sun-washed meadow harbouring a small copse; beyond lay a far view of the river, curling ever wider to the estuary.

On his way back to the Bull, two darkly-clad gentlemen approached him. They were the seconds appointed for the duel. He was pleased to reward them. Glancing back, he wished never again to behold that field of fate, where he had been on the swordpoint of a loathsome experience.

The azure sky and golden embrace of autumn promised a fair ride back to London, every step a trace nearer to his long-awaited meeting with Sophie on the morrow.

CHAPTER SEVENTEEN

London, Grosvenor Square

Sophie lay back upon her pillow and raised her eyes to the pale-green silk canopy of her bed, pleated and embroidered with several cherubs cavorting among flower-garlands. She pondered the bizarre sequence of events that had affected her life since returning to the manor house. She felt as helpless as those few cherubs that sought a hold on the garlands but were left floundering, with no alternative but to accept the imposed circumstances.

The steeplechase and Guy's fate dominated her thoughts. How she longed to see him! His were the only reassurances that would set her mind at ease. She thought of possible London contacts, wondering if Sir Henry Nancarrow was aware of recent events, or whether she could expect Sir Toby to call; but all was speculation. Today she must not dwell upon such things. This was her father's day—the celebration at Carlton House. She rose as Nell entered to serve breakfast and help her prepare for an early-morning dress rehearsal.

Sophie regarded with amazement the dress she was to wear, now displayed on a stand in her dressing-room. A white satin petticoat, draped with silver lace and caught with circlets of blue flowers and lapis lazuli, was topped by a blue velvet train, ornamented with silver, which would fall from her shoulders. A fan and reticule of silver lace, long white gloves and kid slippers, completed the accessories. Her head-dress was a simple bandeau of palest blue, jewelled with lapis lazuli, and surmounted by splendid white ostrich plumes.

On the stand it appeared beautiful and benign, thought Sophie; but then, there were the hoops, which she dreaded. She would have to learn governance of them, with the fanciful attitudes they occasioned. She had laughed at Lady Adela's recounting the disasters befalling those ladies who failed to turn slightly to the side when traversing narrow entrances.

'One must become a feline,' said Lady Adela merrily, 'knowing instinctively the extent of one's whiskers in keeping with the sudden width of the person!' It had all seemed so amusing; but Sophie vowed to wear her hoops with confidence.

Nell came in good time for the dress rehearsal, when the admiral would see the gown for the first time. Somehow, it seemed to Sophie that the finery took charge of her deportment, and earned praise. The admiral stood in place as if he were the Prince Regent, and became the recipient of her much practised curtsy. He smiled his approval, then beckoned her to a side-board where were displayed her gift of the two silver wine-glass coolers.

'I shall treasure these above all, Sophie, knowing of the dangers you overcame in acquiring them for me. Thank you, my dear. We shall never mention that incident again.'

Sophie kissed him. 'It's over,' she said. At the same time, it crossed her mind that she would dearly love to thank that rider who had risked life and limb in stopping the coach.

She returned to her room for a last dressing of her hair. Her heart leapt at the summoning call from her father that they must now leave.

* * *

Sophie and the admiral were seated in a window embrasure of the main salon at Carlton House. The presentations to His Royal Highness the Prince Regent had taken place, the event driving all else from Sophie's mind. After the Prince Regent left his apartment, where the admiral had been honoured, he entered the rooms where the general levée was being held. There he moved among the guests receiving salutations, and Sophie was presented to him.

His Royal Highness had smilingly extended a hand to raise her from the sweeping curtsy, and retained his hold while commenting upon the dignified bearing of his newly appointed Admiral of the Blue. He remarked the fine detail of the admiral's full dress uniform and, before proceeding, commented that the changes wrought by himself and his ducal brothers in all Royal Navy Flag Officers' uniforms, recognized their recent glorious victories.

Captain and Mrs Pettit and Lieutenant and Lady Adela Summerson joined them in company with other young naval lieutenants, vying to bring Sophie any titbit of refreshment she desired. She was happy, seated beside her father, enjoying his discourse and subtle wit.

Sophie regarded the scene with wonderment. All were in elegant court dress or brilliant uniforms. The nobility were numerous as were the military. There were from forty to fifty generals, perhaps as many admirals with throngs of officers of other ranks. A myriad glass prisms caught the candlelight, reflecting the richness of the ladies' gowns.

'Even though it is out of Season,' remarked Lady Adela, 'enough of the nobility are here to make it an outstanding occasion.'

'It must be due to the number of generals and admirals honoured today,' mused Sophie, noting that her father was in deep converse with two other admirals.

Suddenly, Captain Pettit was by her side.

'Miss Stapleford,' he said. 'Would you accompany me to greet another of the admiral's guests whose late appearance was unavoidable?'

'Of course,' she said rising, convinced that

the tardy guest was either another young lieutenant or a doddering admiral.

They left the salon and proceeded through grand rooms to the gothic conservatory. It was lit by vast coloured lanterns so highly placed that the colonnaded cloisters were barely discernible in the fractured light. Banks of greenery were everywhere, and a fragrance drifted upon the air. One of the Prince's bands played here but, for the moment, the bandsmen were at refreshment, their instruments at rest.

'Strange,' said Captain Pettit. 'I do not see our guest. Remain here, Miss Stapleford, and I shall look further.'

She halted, staring at the retreating figure of Captain Pettit who did not appear to be looking for anyone at all. She snapped open her fan and was about to follow when a hand touched her shoulder.

'Sophie,' a voice whispered, 'I shall thank you again and again, and again.'

A heightening delight surged through her as she turned and beheld Guy seriously regarding her. He was a heart-stopping sight, resplendent in full black court dress, his coat embroidered in gold.

'Oh, Guy,' she breathed. 'I have so longed to see you. I had no option but to leave after the race and was so happy . . .'

He gently placed a finger upon her lips.

'Hush,' he said. 'Hear me, now. Do you not

think I have longed to see you? I left Adversane with one purpose, to hasten to you and declare that which my guardianship would not permit. I love you and wish to make you my countess. Such a permanent and desirable bond I yearn to undertake.'

His words tumbled about her ears, for she could hardly believe they had been spoken. She felt incapable of reply, wishing to hold the moment in isolation, precious to herself.

Guy drew her into his arms and, tilting her chin, whispered:

'What have you to say to that, my comely little filly?'

'I have loved you since first you came to the manor house.'

His sea-grey eyes glinted silver. He placed a kiss upon her lips and her response drew forth another and yet another with gathering fervour until, aware of returning musicians and others in the shadowed conservatory, he was obliged to release her. Resting her hand upon his arm, he led her proudly towards the bright and noisy salon, their footsteps moving in unison and hearts beating responsively.

As if in a dream she rejoined her father, who greeted Guy with great warmth, smiling broadly.

'Admiral Sir John Stapleford,' said Guy, inclining his head. 'Would you do me the honour of receiving me tomorrow to pursue some urgent matters concerned with my erstwhile ward, Miss Stapleford?'

Seeing his daughter's radiance, the admiral replied:

'I shall await your call with the greatest pleasure, my lord.'

The rapturous looks, whispered endearments, the furtive brushing of lips on cheek and hand, so delicately accomplished, left the admiral in no doubt of the tenor of the earl's appointment on the morrow.

The next morning, Sophie watched Guy's arrival from an upper landing. He was divested of his cloak, hat and cane and turned to follow the footman to the main salon. For some reason, he looked up and directed a kiss to her with a graceful gesture of his hand.

She counted the moments before receiving a summons to join her father and Guy. She hugged a joyous Nell, and went down the stairs with a sprightliness in her step and in her heart.

Both gentlemen rose as she entered. The admiral came towards her.

'Guy has told me about the steeplechase, Sophie,' he said, embracing her. 'He says you alone saved Adversane. We are both overcome with pride in your courage and endeavour; but appalled to think of the dangers and risks you took.'

'Never again!' said Guy, smiling and clasping both her hands. He led her to a chair, where he knelt to place a diamond-and-sapphire ring upon her finger. Kissing her ringed hand, he proposed a Christmas wedding to be solemnized in Adversane church. She did not utter a word; her rapturous countenance and tears of happiness were answer enough, and held Guy spellbound.

That evening the admiral hosted a party to celebrate the occasion. Hastily summoned friends of Guy and the admiral were happy to come. Champagne flowed, with Sophie herself assisting and chatting to Guy's London friends. She was particularly pleased to meet Lieutenant Jack Watts, whom she had singled out to ask certain questions about her rescue from the coach. His replies confirmed all she had suspected.

During the next weeks, Guy proudly escorted Sophie to the opera, the theatre and to several salons held by the formidable ladies of the London *ton*. She charmed them all, and invitations arrived daily. Most had to be refused, since the admiral's official duties ceased and he was now ready for a return to Adversane.

The Manor House, Adversane

It took but three days for the admiral's countenance to reflect the peace of homecoming. He walked with the dogs every day, then retreated to the captain's room, now called the admiral's room, where he wrote letters and reports, and entertained Guy on his visits to Sophie. Guy made it clear he regarded her as his helpmate in every respect, and discussed his plans for the estate with both Sophie and her father.

It was Guy who suggested that brave little Jet should be put out to grass for the rest of his life. He had recovered well, and Sophie visited him every day. She was delighted when Seb brought over a beautiful grey gelding named Sonnet, a gift from Guy.

When Sophie learned that Sir Toby and Beth were to visit Guy, she suggested extending their stay so that they could meet her father. He readily agreed. Her approaching marriage raised questions, the answers to which she felt only Beth, in her wisdom, could provide.

They arrived in their own carriage, with Guy as their outrider, for an evening repast. Conversation abounded about the steeplechase during the serving of dessert wine and sweetmeats.

'I have received good news from Sir Henry,' said Guy. 'Six prominent banking-houses in London hold considerable sums to my credit. Thus The Skull has paid his gambling debt.'

They voiced wonder at this, since Sir Toby had had his doubts.

'After the race, they melted away,' he said, 'there was no approach. I was sorry to hear about Mayo; he just rode on, you know, and no one knows his whereabouts. It's said he could not sustain the shame of losing to a female rider.'

Sophie withdrew with Beth, leaving the gentlemen to their port. Beth embraced her.

'Welcome to our family, Sophie.'

They engaged in intense and intimate discussions, until the gentlemen joined them. Soon Sir Toby and Beth left for Rothervale, and Guy and Sophie waved them farewell from the porch.

A solitary lantern yielded a loop of golden light; but the air was chill. Sophie shivered, and turned to enter the house, but Guy roughly pulled her to him, wrapping his cloak around her. She closed her eyes and leaned against his breast, feeling his lips upon her hair. There they remained in shared silence, only the gently stirring trees accompanied the throbbing of hearts.

'Darling Sophie,' whispered Guy, 'I often think of your song, "Love's Measure". Surely, the measure of love is that which you are willing to give up for it. You delayed going to your father's side, staying to win the race and delivering me from ruination.'

Sophie smiled. 'But Jack Watts revealed that you were willing to risk your life for me, in stopping the coach and challenging Anton.'

'A full measure, then,' he sighed, holding her closer. He suddenly sought her lips and kissed her with a passion reflecting need, revealing the fever in his blood, which left her breathless.

Spent of breath himself, Guy murmured: 'When we first met, by this very porch, you told me you were chasing dreams. Do you remember?'

She nodded, still bewitched by the wonder and intensity of his kiss.

'Sophie, my love, save your dreams for me to fulfil!'

She knew that was a certainty.

EPILOGUE

From *THE COURT COMPANION*, AUGUST 1818

"The Earl and Countess of Adversane officiated at the opening of the newly built hamlet of Nether Cherry, which was also honoured by the presence of the Lords Lieutenant of the Counties of Hampshire and Sussex. A superb banquet followed at Adversane House, when the earl donated framed watercolour paintings by Dorothy Lachbone, featuring scenes of the old hamlet, to furnish the new school.

A wonderful evening of music ensued, presented by Maestro Basilio Bordoni of the Italian Opera in London, at which the soloists were the soprano, Rosa Bordoni, and the young Miss Harriet Dallimore making her debut as a pianist.

The earl and countess were accompanied by their young son, Rossington John, the Viscount Saxenford.

To the delight of the earl, the countess is again able to attend such functions after the birth of their second child, a daughter, the Lady Elizabeth May de Grais."